I0547199

DEATH STICKS A
Pixie

NORMA'S CLEANING SERVICE
BOOK 3

ELIZABETH GUIZZETTI

Edited by Joe Dacy
Cover and Interior Illustrations by Elizabeth Guizzetti

This is a work of fiction. Names, characters, businesses, places, events
and incidents are products of the author's imagination or used in a
fictitious manner. Any resemblance to actual persons, living or dead, or
actual events is purely coincidental.

Printed in the United States of America

Paperback ISBN-13: 978-1-950708-30-7
Ebook ISBN-13: 978-1-950708-31-4

This book is dedicated to loving families,
However they are formed.

Happy Holidays

Dear Readers:

ONE OF THE LITTLE KNOWN FACTS ABOUT *Death Sticks a Pixie* is its outline was for the fourth book in the series rather than the third. This was simply an issue of learning about cat cafés opening in America, I knew I wanted to place the murder mystery in a cat café — which was a great excuse to go check out a cat café or several. There was always a pixie victim, though I admit I was wrong on who the murderer was. I hope it keeps you guessing till the end.

As I have mentioned previously I am creating second editions of the first three books in the *Norma's Cleaning Service* series in order to complete the series. While I normally don't like to retread stories, this series stopped going to plan years ago! It seemed to me a huge part of the problem was I had tried to write it as a *Paper Flower Consortium Universe Book*, rather than to just tell the books by Norma's perspective. The largest difference between this book and the first edition is that these books were originally released in third person. Note I did not way written, because I was fighting the tendency to go into Norma's perspective constantly. In order the novellas in the series so far:

Book 1: *Death Pulls a Stake Out*
Book 2: *Death Hears a Siren*
Book 3: *Death Sticks a Pixie*

And now that I finished with the second editions, there will be more *Norma's Cleaning Service* on the way!

I want to thank Joe Dacy, who edited the first edition of this book. And thanks to my husband, Dennis, who has supported me in all my writing. And thank you to all the fans

who have encouraged the Paper Flower Consortium to grow.
I could not do it without you.

I hope you enjoy it!

-Elizabeth

December 5, 2019

THURSDAY

Chapter 1

10:43 AM

I AM THE VAMPIRE, NORMA MAE ROLLINS. And I was asleep in my bed when my phone announced a text. With a sleepy groan, I snuggled deeper between the smooth cotton sheets. I covered my head under the thick quilt which my beloved ancestor, Jakub Bankier, nee Petruescu Christian, made for me in an intricate compass rose pattern in the unvampiric shades of blue and yellow. The phone sounded a second time.

My sleepy mind still did not recognize it as a text. I did not want to get up, but believing it was my alarm, I jumped out of bed. I had so much to do.

Half-asleep, I removed a set of guest bedding from the linen closet and put it in the washer. Like most vampires, I enjoyed a certain neatness and order in my home, but Derrik Miller, the vampire who created the vampire who created me, was coming over. We had a busy weekend planned.

I wanted the guest bathroom and kitchen spotless and all the laundry done before work tonight. Then I planned to hit a club and tap a willing victim's neck.

Tomorrow at twilight, Derrik's enthralled human would drop him off downtown. We planned to go Christmas shopping, or at the very least, enjoy Christmas decorations while Derrik agonized over what to give his wife, Pascaline. My eternal girlish form meant it was unlikely I would ever have such a concern, but according to Derrik, it was hard to find the perfect Christmas gift after a hundred seventy years of marriage. Since Pascaline recently awoke from torpor, he wanted to ensure this year was special. Pascaline and I had attended movies, art museums, and other social activities together. He wanted insider information. Pascaline never had such concerns, she had a knack for picking out perfect gifts. (I've seen the present, I think he'll love it!)

After the stores closed, we planned to visit Gingerbread Lane at the Sheraton Grand, which was open until 11 PM on Fridays. Then we will walk along streets enjoying the lights toward South Lake Union to see boats lit up for the Christmas Parade. Since Derrik rarely left the coven, I could not wait to show him how South Lake Union had grown. A neighborhood in renewal, many apartment windows were decorated, and lighted cranes dotted the skyline.

Due to my work, I knew what late-night clubs were vampire-friendly. We would stop in one or two. Derrik did not normally mingle in such places. They were too noisy, and he didn't appreciate modern dancing or contemporary music. However, he did enjoy sampling holiday drinks.

Through the short-day hours, Derrik would stay over at my apartment. While we hung my lights and garlands, he would fret about how unvampiric it was. When we wrapped presents, Derrik would tell me, as he did every year, how he and the other elder vampires at the Paper Flower Consortium didn't celebrate the secular festivities of Christmas until I came into their existence. Born in poverty during the Victorian era, Derrik attended services hoping to receive alms if the factory where he worked was closed. As a vampire, Christmas was a feast day. He and the other elder vampires spent the night and day in adulatory worship of God and Jesus. (Except our honored brother, Bai Xiao who is a Buddhist.)

Every year, Derrik's story seemed to grow sappier as he skated by the difficult realities. In truth, he had been at his wit's end. He and Pascaline were willing to try anything to comfort the despondent, frightened, and angry fourteen-year-old me. Ripped out of my human life by his Firstborn, Bill, and then taken away from Bill on the night of his execution, it took me months to acclimatize to the coven. The elder vampires suggested some well-known human traditions might offer comfort and cheer. It sort of worked. And I learned I could trust Derrik - a tiny Christmas miracle for the circumstances.

Forcing my eyes open, I went to my reading alcove off the living room. While some species would love the natural sunlight the bay window provided, I had covered it with internal shutters painted white and thick blackout curtains so no light could get in. I removed the carved wood statuette of a Sasquatch, a basket of coasters, and a short pile of books off the oak casket which doubled as a coffee table. It bothered Derrik that I slept in a queen-sized bed rather than a coffin—like a normal vampire. However, I kept a casket for him or Pascaline to sleep in when they stayed overday.

I opened the lid. The scent of lemon, lavender, and cedar greeted me. I removed the sachets and cedar blocks and put them in the kitchen cupboards and left the casket to air. The casket set on the thick wool rug, two leather upholstered chairs, thick curtains, and books of all genres made the reading alcove the most vampire-like space in my home.

The plan was on Saturday evening, I would drive Derrik back to the coven. Derrik's enthralled human had picked out a tree and bought a case of spiced wine. Derrik would mix cow's blood with the wine, and we would decorate his Christmas tree. Since he would go to a vampire-friendly club, I would dutifully attend Mass and Fellowship with him, Pascaline, and their other offspring. Then there would be Sunday morning supper, board games, and Pascaline would play songs on her piano.

Still groggy, I went into the guest bathroom. I set out the bottle of Windex, Method bathroom cleaner, bleach, sponges, and paper towels on the bathroom counter. Not wanting to damage my manicure, I put on vinyl gloves. I dutifully checked the corners of the ceiling for discolored paint and dabbed it with diluted bleach, fearing mold. I bought the mid-century condo in the seventies. It had charm, but it also had old drywall.

From my bedroom, my phone binged again.

Another bing followed quickly. This time I recognized it as a text.

Derrik or Pascaline would not text as they felt clumsy with the technology, but Derrik's Secondborn, Ryan, might.

Or Carlos, my best friend and employee, might be dealing with another rotting body part.

Or it might be a job.

I tossed my sponge into the sink and snapped off my

vinyl gloves. I rinsed my hands. I traversed my cold tile floor to the hardwoods and picked up my phone off my dresser. 10:43 AM. No wonder I was so sleepy. I had only been asleep for forty minutes.

The text came my down-the-street neighbor, Weyna Bayard Pollenjacket, a pixie who ran the pixie and cat café: The Cat's Pajamas. **I need help, please come over.**

Emergency.

Please answer.

Me: **Just got your text. I'll be over in five.**

I looked at my not-clean bathroom and sighed.

I crept towards the east window. The immolating sun lightened the wall under my blackout curtains. It was a sunny day. *Ugh.* While Seattle winters were known to be mild, it needed to rain in December or there would be another drought. Like all vampires and other long-lived species, I worried about global warming. Also, I didn't like the sun.

I rewashed my hands and slathered sunscreen on my face, neck, and hands. I removed my pajamas and threw them directly into the washing machine.

I quickly pulled on jeans, a fresh t-shirt, socks, and sneakers. I grabbed a hoodie and cap off the hook. Locking my apartment tight, I pulled the hoodie over my head as I slipped down my apartment steps. Before I hit the vestibule, I covered my hair with the baseball cap and pulled the hood up.

I walked carefully down the street in the shade of the building. The sun was in the east, but my north-facing building's awning blocked most of the sun. I dashed between the open alley way and around the block to the café.

Weyna flew towards me.

Most pixies were a little taller than an adult vampire-sized (or human-sized) hand including fingers, and Weyna was about average-sized. Her brilliant blue eyes matched the sky and her pink complexion looked even more rosy in the cold morning. Weyna had a few lines around her eyes, but her cheeks were smooth and plump. She looked like Mrs. Claus in her red and white dress with a tiny sprig of holly as an apron. Her curly pink and silver hair was neatly braided, but the ends frizzed in the winter air. Her wings fluttered fast. Her heart quivered faster.

"I heard from a little bird, you've been solving murders."

Norma's Cleaning Service was initially for vampires when hunting got a little messy, but my company now ran all types of errands for the supernatural community. After a few murders, Derrik suggested I procure Private Investigator licenses to remain on the right side of the law. I took his advice.

"Yes, we charge..."

Weyna's face fell. "I can't pay you, at least right away. The café is barely staying afloat as it is."

I pinched my lips shut. I hated turning people away who needed help, besides there was always something I could use.

An old dream slipped into my brain.

Maybe, pixies knew magic that could help with learning to alter my shell. Perhaps I could leave my fourteen-year-old body behind. I didn't want to be really different; I loved my "life" as a vampire, but a fully adult body would be nice. And if I couldn't have that, perhaps I could change into a bat or learn to fly or...

I always wanted to turn into a bat or a mist like in the movies. Werewolves could live both as humans and wolves. Werebears could live both as humans and bears. I once met a witch who was transformed into a cat, but I never met a vampire who could turn into anything except what they were. Of course, it might be that truly ancient vampires might be able to transform, but the oldest vampires in Seattle were only five centuries. And the few ancients over in Bellevue never tried. (I had asked.)

"Well, maybe we can work something out — a payment plan or make a trade? What's the problem?" I said.

"Persimmon is dead," Weyna said.

"Oh my God!" I said with practiced emotion but thought *you should have led with that.*

I had met Persimmon Olive a few times when I had stopped in for coffee. The woman seemed to be a happy young pixie who liked her job at the café.

"Poor little sprite is engaged to be married and trying to save up for the wedding. Poor girl." Tears drifted up to Weyna's eyes. Pixie voices were high, tinny, and due to their comparative size, also relatively quiet. Weyna's choking sobs made her even harder to understand. A passing car completely drowned her out. Trying to speak outside was futile.

"Let's go inside. Tell me everything," I said.

"What?" Weyna replied with a sniff.

I was too tired to argue or explain. I pushed my way through the front door of the café with a nod towards

Weyna's adult daughter, Meadow, and their employee, Airie Flaxen. Dressed like Santa's elves, they sat on the window box decorated with Christmas lights. To the unbelieving masses passing by, they just looked like pretty Christmas fairies decorating the store front.

As I knew they would, the pixies followed me inside. The smell of coffee filled my nostrils from the bags of roasted beans. *God, I need a cup.*

I pulled out my phone and snapped a quick photo.

"Who found her?" I asked the pixies who crowded the doorway.

"My mom and I when we got here," Meadow said. Thankfully, her small voice clearly audible in the empty café.

The younger Pollenjacket was a twee little pixie with her mother's eyes and her father's green complexion. She had braced against the cold in a long woolen vest over her Santa's elf costume, and her dark curly hair was covered in a ski cap with a large silver button. I didn't know if it was really silver or even metal, but I was allergic to silver like all vampires of my bloodline.

"We found blood on Captain Fluffy McWhiskers," Weyna cried.

"What if she killed her!" Airie shouted. About the same age as Meadow, Airie was just as slender and pretty as Meadow her complexion was icy blue, and her hair was silver.

"The girls won't work around a pixie-eater, not that I blame them, but we make so much on the Instagram channel. Fluffy is one of our best cats. She's never so much swatted at us. I can't have a pixie and cat café without pixies and cats."

Weyna kept crying.

"It's Thursday night! We can't have the café closed tonight and tomorrow! The college kids will be leaving soon for winter break. We'll have no customers.

"We get so many college kids who miss their pets, they are too young for clubs, but perfect for us," Meadow said to me, while trying to calm her mother. "Norma will help us. She helps everyone."

I sighed. "And when exactly did you find Persimmon?"

Weyna sniffed. "A bit before 10:30. Airie came in what? Five minutes after. I pushed both girls out and texted you."

Thinking of the vampire-sized employees (probably humans, but one never knew until I met them) who served the humans who patronized the café, I asked, "When do the rest of your employees come in?"

"The first shift comes in at noon. We feed the cats and get ready, then we open once we have the big people to keep up appearances," Meadow said.

"Okay. I'm going to take a look," I said. "Are you okay in the doorway? I can let you into my apartment if you need a place to rest."

"We'll be fine," Meadow said.

I pushed a chair over to them so they could rest. "Don't touch anything."

Chapter 2

10:47 AM

B EFORE I DID ANYTHING ELSE, I TEXTED Carlos: **There's been a death at Cat's Pajamas. I'm on the case. Want to join in?**

Carlos loved cats. He would probably be interested in missing a day's sleep to prove a cat's innocence. Still, I didn't expect an answer right away. A shade (also known as a revenant or zombie) wasn't disturbed by the sun. However, since his transformation, Carlos worked nights and hung out with the other vampires in my family. He kept a similar schedule.

I attempted to determine the entire crime scene, including paths of entry and exit. I would need to contain the area, but the pixies had already been in there for fifteen minutes before I arrived. I had already stepped through the front door, so I might have tainted the evidence.

Unless there was another way in and out?

"Besides the front door, what other doors are there?" I asked.

"There's the emergency exit, but that's kept locked. It only can be opened from the inside," Meadow said in a business-like manner. "And there's a door in the back of the office which leads to the alley. We also keep that door locked."

"You don't take garbage out that way?"

"No, sometimes homeless people hang out in the alley," Airie said.

"What about windows?"

"There's a vent window in the bathrooms, but it's too small of an opening for a big person to get through," Meadow said.

"Do you have gendered bathrooms?"

"No, only two single bathrooms. The vent windows are small with bars over the glass."

Whoever hurt Persimmon must have entered and exited the crime scene through the front door, emergency door, or back door through the office. *Unless the perpetrator was a pixie or other small individual though the window?* I thought.

My sneakers squeaked across the polished concrete floors as I moved further into the café. I didn't know if humans or pixies could smell the three resident cats from the retail side, which stayed in the glassed-in cat lounge, but I could.

I took a photo of a melted puddle of something looked sticky. Melted caramel maybe or jam, but it was a weird bluish color.

As I drew closer to the coffee counter, the grassy and spicy scents of the wall of teas overtook the smell of cats. Bottles of syrups, hazelnut, mint, vanilla, and many others, lined the counter beside chocolate, white chocolate, and caramel sauces. Three blenders stood sentry beside the bottles as the coffee house made a lot of sweet drinks to fill college students with caffeine and sugar. Beside the faux wood espresso machine stood a collection of mostly clean the frothing pitchers.

I smothered my impulses to wash them. No wonder Weyna came in early to ensure the café's cleanliness. The night staff wasn't as diligent as the owners.

Over the counter, a chalkboard menu was festooned with pink and red sparkling garland. There were regular espresso drinks, monthly specials which sounded like sugar bombs, and a list of pastries all with standard Seattle prices. A tiny sign under the counter proclaimed Cat's Pajama's proudly partnered with Anna's Pâtisserie. This wasn't surprising many small cafés purchased wholesale pastries from one of the bakeries who worked out of the commercial spaces in Sodo but couldn't afford their own storefront.

Next to the register, the tip jar was full of coins and small bills. *Hmmm. Didn't that get counted with the shift change?*

Also on the counter were plastic trays filled with fresh delicious-looking pastries not yet put away.

"I'm guessing you don't have a breakfast rush here," I called.

"No, it's quick lunches, mid-afternoon snacks, and dessert," Meadow said.

"What are your hours?"

"Monday through Thursday, noon to 9:30. Friday and Saturday noon to 10:30. We are closed on Sundays."

Most of the retail area consisted of six metal garden-style tables set with two chairs each. "Do people sit here or go in with the cats?"

"Most go in with the cats, but food has to be eaten out here. Health codes. Plus, it's safer for the cats," Weyna said.

I nodded and made a non-committal um-hum sound to acknowledge her words.

The west wall was covered in shelves of cat mugs, cat stuffed animals, cat shirts, cat-shaped chocolates and other merchandise. In the corner closest to the street window, a small giving tree was decorated with cat garland and paper ornaments with pet drive information on it. Underneath were three large boxes of pet food and pet supplies for the charity.

Looking at the Christmas tree, my mind flew to Ryan, Derrik's Secondborn, and Fern, his future immortal bride. They had always been pleasant enough when their orbits crossed mine, but in years past, I hadn't given him a present, primarily because he never got me anything. However, recently, Ryan and Fern became much more friendly. (I rescued Ryan from being immolated and proved his innocence after one of their honored coven brothers were staked.) Ryan was a Christian, but I wasn't sure if Fern even celebrated Christmas. I would have to ask. Derrik would know.

I pushed the thought out of my head. *How can I think of Christmas shopping at a time like this?*

At the condiment station, beside the packets of sugar, shakers of cinnamon, and cocoa, a body no bigger than my hand was impaled on a straw. Poor Persimmon.

I took several pictures. My vampire sight saw a deep scratch on her tiny cheek. Her sparkling, rainbow dress was ripped open. I understood why Weyna's first thought was one of the cats batted her onto the straw, but that doesn't seem possible. Enough force to impale a pixie on a straw should have shown more damage or at least more blood.

All three cats were in the glass-walled lounge. A bloody pawprint was smeared across the window. I peaked inside.

The walls were dominated by a painted mural featuring cats in pajamas running along rainbows, riding an orca, waving from a ferry, and climbing the Spaceneedle. A plate rail allowed the real cats to walk where they wished. There were also several perches covered in carpet and scratching posts.

A sunbeam slashed across the cat lounge.

"Can someone drop the shade?"

I snapped another photo and walked to the cat lounge door. It wasn't locked. I was greeted by a jubilant chorus of meow meow meow.

A brown cat jumped down from her perch and rubbed her head against my ankles. Smiling, I knelt down and ran my fingers through the soft brown fur. The cat purred as I picked her up. I rubbed the cat's legs and taking care to check the brown cat's paws for blood or other foreign matter. I didn't feel anything.

The cat on the scratching post meowed in complaint as the eastern window's sunbeam disappeared as Airie lowered the shade.

I set the purring cat down and went to the next cat, who lay on a scratching post. I picked up a feather pole. The cat rolled over to catch it. I checked her paws. Though she playfully bit me when I touched her legs, I didn't see any blood on the second cat's paws.

I checked the final cat, a multi-colored cat who had a slash of blood in her fur.

This one must be Captain Fluffy McWhiskers. The blood didn't seem to be in her claws only on the right front leg. Still, just as a vampire might be a danger to a human, a cat might be a deadly creature to a pixie.

"Merow." The cat from the scratching post flicked a toy towards me.

I bent down and reached for it. In a furry blur, the cat quickly grabbed it and jumped up to a higher perch.

I glanced out and saw the pixies watching. No time to play with cats when there was a murder to solve. I snapped photos of the three cats. I was glad I called in Carlos. If one of the three was a pixie killer, they would need a new home.

Careful to not let the cats escape and cause a panic, I backed out of the lounge. I crossed the café to the pixies, still in the doorway. "I'll figure out who or what killed Persimmon, clean up the mess, and I know how you can pay me."

"But we really have no extra money right now." Meadow's wings fluttered quickly.

"I understand," I said. "And this is a longshot, but do pixies know any transformation magic?"

"Transformation magic?" Weyna repeated.

"Yes. Do you know to change me into something else? I've always wanted to learn to change into a bat."

Airie rolled her eyes. Meadow dropped her face to her hands.

Weyna briefly glanced towards her daughter than looked away.

I sensed Weyna almost told me what I wanted to hear

to ensure my assistance, but then she glanced at her daughter again. "No, sorry. We don't know that type of magic. The best we could do is a bat glamour, but then you'd just look like a gigantic bat walking around."

"What about flying?" I asked.

"What?" Airie said. "You're heavy and don't have wings. How would you fly? And don't even say pixie dust."

"I don't know how to fly, that's why I was asking," I said, keeping my voice calm and gentle. "Alright then, if there isn't any magic you might trade, what about a cappuccino for me and an Americano for Carlos before work for the next year and as much coffee as we need to stay awake today. Finally, I could use an all-age place to hunt on Friday nights for however many years, you are open."

Weyna gasped.

"You can't kill our customers," Meadow said.

"If I leave with your customers, they'll always come back happy and alive," I promised.

That was a lie of omission. I did kill people, but only when my victim was a fiend who beat their children, kicked puppies, or otherwise harmed those weaker than themselves. I doubted such people would patronage a cat café more than once. *And if they did, the pixies would want me to kill them.*

"Other vampires will come here?" Weyna asked, her voice becoming stronger and less shaky.

"Maybe from my bloodline, but only to visit the cats and drink coffee, not to hunt."

"How can you be sure?" Meadow tugged on her blouse.

"I'd mark the building."

"Mark the building?" Weyna glanced at her daughter

again.

"With one of my protection wards. Only vampires and witches can see them. Everyone in the community knows I live around here, and no vampire would dare anger me. If you don't like those terms, I also accept credit cards," I said.

Another half-truth.

I would put an enchanted protection ward on the building, and I was one of the most feared vampires in Seattle. However, the truth was, I kept my ear to the ground to know which vampires were hunting and where. Most vampires play hunted. They wanted to be welcomed into vampire-friendly clubs, so they didn't kill the clientele. Those who hunted to kill pursued easier and less morally taxing prey than kitty-loving students. They went south of downtown in less-congested industrial neighborhoods. Capitol Hill was too crowded.

I added a final condition. "You will ensure none of your employees try to take photos of me or speak about me on social media or at all. If they do, I will be forced to protect myself."

"But everyone knows of Norma's Cleaning Service," Airie said.

"Yet, no one talks about it on social media. Tell them I'm a Luddite. Tell them I'm part of a *Fight Club*. I don't care. If you put me in danger, I will protect myself."

Airie nodded.

Meadow and Weyna spoke to each other in quiet words. I heard every high-pitched whisper, but I waited tranquilly while they discussed it.

"We accept your terms," Meadow said.

"And you're sure you want me to do this?" I asked.

"Why?" Weyna asked.

"Someone's always hurt when a murder is solved. If you murdered her, or your daughter…"

"But we didn't," Meadow said quickly.

"Good."

I didn't trust or distrust their words. My long existence had shown me that people of all species were capable of anything. "I need to run home and get my kit, but I'll be right back. Try not to touch anything until I get pictures and fingerprints."

Another thought slipped into my mind. "Have you contacted Persimmon's fiancée?"

"Yes. We called my husband. They work together. Craig will inform her," Weyna said.

"Then they will be coming here?" I asked.

"I would presume so," Weyna said.

No one should see their loved ones impaled on a pink compostable straw. My first job was to clean the body. I took one more shot of the café so I might see if anything had been moved when I was gone.

Chapter 3

11:02 AM

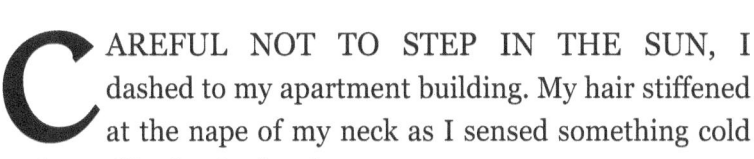

CAREFUL NOT TO STEP IN THE SUN, I dashed to my apartment building. My hair stiffened at the nape of my neck as I sensed something cold and antediluvian in the air.

I glanced around; I was the only undead creature on the street. *Calm down. I know how I get when I don't get a full day's sleep. It's probably just an ancient vampire staying in a nearby hotel.*

From my apartment, I could see downtown to the Hyatt at Olive 8. Down Pike and Union streets, there were even more choices. Plenty of well-healed vampires loved the Four Seasons, Hilton, and other upscale chains. Though the Paper Flower Consortium ran a reasonably-priced extended-stay hotel for visiting vampires, it was only a three-star. Ancient vampires with money preferred to be closer to the downtown business core rather than Georgetown. B&B's in the old Victorian mansions by Volunteer Park catered to the vampire with more conventional tastes.

Get a grip. They are probably in town to do some Christmas shopping too.

With a final glance over my shoulder, I slipped my

key into the door to the garage. I peeped in the corners and between cars, unable to shake the feeling that something dead was nearby. I wasn't afraid of the homeless humans who sometimes found temporary shelter between the vehicles or hidden behind the dumpster, but I hated the smell of urine that tainted in the concrete. I hurried to my van to get my kit and camera, relocked my vehicle, and ran up the stairs to the condo careful no one followed me inside.

I swapped the sheets to the dryer and put the quilt which Derrik liked in the washer. I gathered more supplies. I put a small notebook and pen in my jeans pocket. I would also dictate to my phone, but found sometimes writing notes jogged my mind.

I grabbed a never-used laced-edged silk handkerchief from my top drawer. I took a hand-carved wooden box off my shelf. The box was fancier than the rocks, which were just things I liked to touch. I dumped the rocks in a mixing bowl and took the box with me. I cut a few blossoms off the fresh flowers which I had gotten from the market and set them inside.

I didn't know any vampires who were experts on pixie anatomy, but Derrik might. However, he was a man of schedule. He would be in bed at this hour. It was pretty late for Pascaline too.

Agata, the eldest vampire in Seattle and the CEO of the Paper Flower Consortium, might still be up. While not an expert of pixies, she was a midwife and had a vast array of medical knowledge. Moreover, Agata always encouraged my enterprises.

She answered on the third ring. "Ahoy, hoy, Norma.

Why are you calling so late, dear? Should I send a car for you?"

"No, *Bunică*, I'm fine. I have a medical question. Were you still up?"

"Indeed. Jakub and I have so many Christmas, Chanukah, Winter, and New Year's Greetings to write and send for the Consortium."

Agata sent Christmas cards to Christian vampire and witches, Chanukah to those of the Jewish faith, Winter cards to those who followed the nature religions, and New Years Greetings to everyone else. She hand wrote messages to everyone on her list. "Is your question about vampires, witches, or humans?"

"Pixies."

There was a slight pause in Agata's voice. "I don't know much about pixies," she said.

"I just need some general anatomy," I said.

"Hold on, I have a book."

I heard Agata say something to someone, presumably Jakub. Their marriage was arranged in medieval Moldavia for political reasons, but they respected each other and grew to love each other. In fact, Jakub loved his wife so much that after Agata was attacked and became a vampire, he asked her to change him. The rest of the vampires in the Paper Flower Consortium were their descendants. Derrik was Jakub's Secondborn.

Jakub got on the phone. "Hello, Norma, how is my favorite vampire cleaner-slash-private detective?"

"I'm fine, Jakub. How are you?" (Though Agata loved being my *Bunică*, Jakub preferred being addressed by his given name.)

"Good. Getting ready for tax season and helping your grandmother with all this correspondence. Sometimes I feel the vampires' holiday cards fund the post office." He paused. "So, another murder?"

"Looks like it. I might be doing a barter to solve the crime through."

"Just bring in your receipts same as always, I'll figure it out for you. Here is your *Bunică*. She worries as does Derrik, be safe."

A former knight and general of the calvary, Jakub never spoke of his own worries only Agata's or Derrik's.

"So, honey, what do you want to know?" Agata asked.

"Do pixies have a rib cage?" I asked.

"Most certainly."

"Is the ribcage weak enough that a compostable-plastic straw might go through them? The pixie in question looks to be impaled on the straw."

"Hmmm," Agata said, "Anything moving at a fast-enough velocity could be impaled on something, I would suppose, but those are supernatural speeds. Compostable straws can be very flimsy. They soften quickly."

"Can I email you pictures and notes after I finish cleaning up the body."

"Please do."

"How much later will you be up?" I asked.

"My curiosity is piqued. I shall not go to my coffin until I see the photos. Be careful, Norma," Agata said. "Pixies are small, but they do have more power than most give them credit for."

"I will be," I said.

Yet they don't know how to transform me into a bat, I thought sadly. *Of course, neither does any vampire I have ever met.*

Chapter 4

11:17 AM

I RETURNED TO THE CAFÉ. THE SHADES HAD been opened again, but the pixies were still sitting on the chair near the door. Sunlight gleamed into the southeast window of the café. Well, I would fix that soon enough. Everything felt like it was happening too fast, but I knew I was just tired. Sleep hygiene was more important as one got older.

Careful to not step directly into the beam, I took several photos around the café and quickly drew the shades closed.

The criminologist, Edmond Locard, said: "Every contact leaves its trace."

I understood this theory and used it extensively in my work to make messy hunts and other crimes disappear. After I became a licensed Private Investigator, I became more serious about procedure. I felt no guilt having spent years protecting the guilty, but never ever wanted to do anything that might hurt the innocent. I read about police and forensic procedures and spent hours in Derrik's law office looking up cases were evidence was the deciding factor. My cases were often ignored by the human police, as many of my clients, like pixies, didn't officially exist in regards to human law.

My first stop was the condiment counter with Persimmon's body. I went through a similar procedure in every cleanup I did no matter the size or species of the corpse, but since I was also trying to figure out who killed the unfortunate woman, I set up my tripod. I mounted my camera and rotated it so the plane of the image would be parallel to the plane of the countertop. I took one series of pictures without a scale and then placed a plastic scale parallel to the side of each shoe print. I took several more photographs of each footprint, an overall shot, medium shot, and closeups. I set the flash at a 45-degree angle from the print and fired from three different positions with 100 degrees separation between each one.

I applied fingerprint dust and ran tape strips over the countertops, several blurred and partial fingerprints came up. However, one of the clearer prints was of a cat's paw.

I sniffed the tape for smells of sweat, but there wasn't a single or even most potent fragrance. Too many people have touched the counter, the straw container, the sugar packets to get a strong impression. I wasn't sure if this first collection would yield usable evidence or not, but after taking the impressions, I covered them with clear acetate to protect them.

I removed the bent straw with the speared pixie out of the cup and dusted it for prints. I placed it on the counter and carefully took more photos from every available angle. Persimmon was impaled about a third of the way down on the plastic. The inside of the straw was a little bloody, but there were no organs or pieces of flesh. Strange.

I removed the straw from Persimmon's torso,

continuing to take photographs. Her body was in complete rigor. No blood poured out the wound. Persimmon must have been dead for a few hours, at least, probably much later. I would ask Agata if she knew how long rigor mortis lasted in pixies. Body temperature was 19.2 Celsius (66.2 F). It was probably a little colder than that in the restaurant.

"What is your thermostat set to?" I asked.

"It automatically drops to 50 degrees at night. It is set to go up to 65 during working hours," Meadow said. "Should I turn it up early?"

"Please," I said.

The dead pixie wore no jewelry. Her long, horizontal-striped rainbow skirts matched her rainbow hair. I looked closer and saw that Persimmon's roots were black. I took a swab from my kit and wiped the pixie's skin. Persimmon's purple glittery makeup exposed fuchsia flesh. Darker pink than Weyna's, but not as violet as the makeup. Wiping some of the foundation away, I saw the darken mottled flesh. Her blood had pooled in Persimmon's feet and calves.

I took a picture of the bloody straw. Other than the blood stains, it looked like a regular compostable straw. I sniffed the end of the straw. It smelled vaguely of iron, grass, and spring flowers. Persimmon must be a vegan. Living in Capitol Hill, I had tasted plenty of human vegans. Glancing to ensure the pixies didn't see, I licked it. Yep, a vegan. I set it a baggie.

I searched for the tiny puddles of blood or flesh with and quickly gathered a few stained sugar packets, which I put in a plastic baggie. I wiped of the small amount of spilled blood from the counter. I emptied the straw container. No blood had reached the bottom of the container. The rest of the straws were clean. I replaced the straws.

Persimmon most likely didn't die impaled on the straw? Or at least not on the condiment counter.

Though versed in many species and religions specific protocols, this was the first time I handled a pixie's body. Fortunately, I had worked for other species who lived by the same nature religion. I wrapped Persimmon's body gently in the silken handkerchief and place her in the hand-carved box and set three blossoms as a pillow. I combed Persimmon's hair into place. I snapped a quick picture.

Then I emailed Agata my photos, observational notes and asked a few questions.

My phone was still in my hand when it binged with an incoming text.

Carlos: **Cat café is in trouble?**

I sent the picture of the cats in the lounge, which I took earlier to Carlos. I sighed in relief. I worked for decades without Carlos but having an extra set of hands and someone to bounce ideas off of was always a help.

Carlos: **Missed the last morning train, I'll need to drive in, where can I park?**

I texted him the address to a fairly reasonable all-day parking lot within a few blocks of the café. Then added: **I'll reimburse the parking. Get a receipt.**

Carlos: **OK. BRT**

Chapter 5

11:45 AM

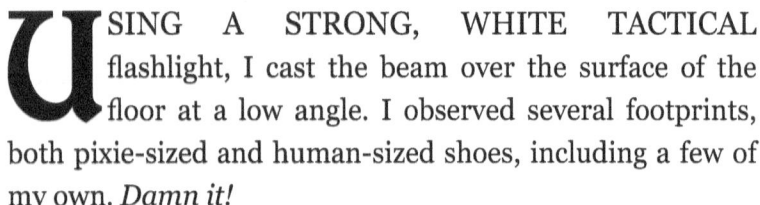

USING A STRONG, WHITE TACTICAL flashlight, I cast the beam over the surface of the floor at a low angle. I observed several footprints, both pixie-sized and human-sized shoes, including a few of my own. *Damn it!*

Annoyed with myself, I moved my tripod and prepared to record the scene in the same manner in which I photographed the counter. "I'm going to need to move the chair over so I can get photos of the door, OK?"

"We can do it." Weyna said. "Where should we be?"

"Just six feet to the right, please. By the tree."

Weyna flicked her fingers. The chair lifted a few inches off the floor and was set by the tree. So Weyna, perhaps all pixies, were telekinetic. Good to know.

After I finished photographing the main entrance, I carefully tried to lift the impressions with fingerprint dust and contact paper. Once the impressions and partials were transferred to the adhesive side of the paper, I covered the impressions with clear acetate to preserve them for later examination. I hurried into the office to repeat the procedures at the back door and fire exit. I needed to know if people used those doors — or if they were always locked as Weyna claimed.

The evidence showed no one went out of or came in the fire door, though plenty walked by it. However, scratches on the tiled floor exposed the backdoor through the office was opened and closed several times and while the retail area was mopped, this back area wasn't.

Interesting. I knew better than to jump to conclusions, as it just might mean one of the employees use the back door to take out the trash or catch a quick smoke break.

At the cat lounge, I photographed and then scratched a bit of dried blood from the window into a baggie. Sniffing it, I discovered it was not pixie blood, but a human who ate way too much sugar. Occupational hazard in a place like this.

I dusted for prints on the door to the cat lounge. Then I washed the door and the windows to the cat lounge.

I went to where I had stepped in the sticky jelly substance. I sniffed it: sweet. I scrapped it into a bag and then mopped the residue off the floor. I studied the glass case, there was no matching residue. Nor was there any of the cleaned dishes. I glanced through the washed dishes, while there were plenty of forks, spoons, and butter knives, there were no sharp knives among the cutlery.

The café was clean enough for now and Persimmon's body was packed for transport, I could relax and get more information from the pixies while I waited for Carlos to arrive.

"If you want to put the pastries in the fridge or the counter, it's fine now," I called to the pixies. "Will you make me a cappuccino and tell me more about Persimmon."

I slid into a wooden chair near the Christmas Tree. The aromatic fresh grounds smelled chocolaty with a hint of cherry.

"Any flavor?" Meadow asked.

"No thanks."

"Sweetener?"

"No."

I closed my eyes for a moment listening to the hiss of the espresso machine and the whine of the milk steamer. I felt as if I might fall asleep. I opened my eyes to the clatter of a saucer followed by a mug which Weyna set on the table in front of me.

"Thank you, Weyna, Meadow," I said reflexively.

The heat felt good on my icy fingers. The cappuccino had a kitten face decorating the foam. I smiled and raised the warm cup to my lips. The coffee was smooth and the milk foam had its natural sweetness.

Meadow created three pixie-sized drinks and the pixies sat on the table with their own cups of what looked like hot chocolate, this close I smelled mint.

"Tell me about Persimmon," I said.

"A nice girl. She's engaged to Basilla who works over at the Conservatory. They were saving up for a wedding." Weyna sniffed and cried into her hot chocolate.

"All our customers love her and tip really big," Meadow said. "Especially during Pride Month. She was great with rainbow glamours."

"Rainbow glamours?" I asked, establishing a mental connection. Pixies were harder to make mental connections with than humans, but I could do it if I concentrated. Their hearts beat too fast to understand their body impulses. Their fluttering wings dampened my ability to read minds. That and getting less than forty minutes of sleep.

Still, I sensed Weyna felt guilty. Airie was worried about losing her job. Meadow was hardest to read. Her main emotion was annoyance by the inconvenience and her mother's sentiments.

"We cast rainbow spells with each cup of coffee," Weyna said. "Hers were the brightest."

"Did she have any problems with anyone?" I asked.

"Not that we ever saw," Airie said. "Everyone loved her."

I could tell that was a lie, but very little else. My face must be showing my disbelief, because Airie kept babbling. "I mean she was a bit exuberant and lively, but always trying to spread positive energy."

"It's one of the reasons she was such a great employee. Always smiling. Someone would have a bad day at school and pop in and she'd be sitting on their shoulder or luring one of the cats to sit on their laps," Weyna said softly.

"Nothing happened recently?"

The three pixie women glanced at each other.

"It doesn't matter how small."

"Well, Weyna had a fight with her," Airie said. "But it wasn't a real fight."

"I think that's one of the reasons my mom's so upset," Meadow said in a false calm voice, but by the way, Meadow's eyes darted towards Airie, I could see she was pissed.

"What happened, Weyna?" I asked.

"You never know when you will say your last words

to someone. I wish mine were kinder." Weyna's stress level pitched her tone even higher.

"What was the argument about?" I pressed my fingers against my cup.

"Time off. She wanted two weeks off after the wedding. We just can't afford to be understaffed once second semester starts. I told her she could have one week plus the weekend and Monday, but I needed her back the next Tuesday."

"It sounds cruel, we know, but we can't be so understaffed," Meadow said.

"I told her if she needed that long, she would need to find another job," Weyna said.

"How did she take that?" I asked.

"She just laughed and flitted off," Weyna said.

"It's bad enough we can barely get the human-sized employees staffed," Meadow said. "But even other pixies don't respect us. Customers don't believe we are the owners."

"What's the pay here?"

"Minimum wage plus the tips are split among the employees."

I suddenly heard an annoyed thought pop in Airie's mind about the tip jar.

"What about the tip jar?" I asked Airie.

The little blue pixie's eyes grew wide. She glanced at Meadow. "Well, some days it just seems a little short."

Interrogating lying witnesses was brutal when I was drowsy. I downed my cappuccino and took a deep breath. I was glad Carlos was on his way. Two sleepy detectives were better than one.

"Any idea who might have taken it?" I asked.

"No," Airie replied. "No one will cop to stealing or tell on the others. I always figured it was one of the big people since they had easier access and it's happened over multiple shifts."

"You don't like working with big people?" I asked directly. It was always good to learn a suspect's prejudices.

"I like it fine. They tend to ignore us since we don't fit into the big person world," Airie said.

"Your customers are primarily big people."

"Yes."

"Why do you work here?" I asked.

"It's a job. Better than working outside in the cold." That was the truth.

I nodded thoughtfully. "Does Persimmon normally work the opening shift?"

"No," Meadow said.

"Oh my flowers, do you think she was killed last night and stayed like that all night?" Weyna wailed into her hands.

"That's what I'm trying to figure out. Were the doors locked when you arrived?"

"Yes," Meadow said.

"And was the alarm activated?"

"I don't know…I don't remember," Weyna said. "Must have been."

"Was anything out of place? Something caught your attention."

"Well, the door to the cat lounge was ajar. Not a lot, but Captain was out on the table. Chocolate and Pirate were cuddled up inside on the big scratching pole. We lured Captain back in, then we saw the blood," Meadow said.

"May I have the names of all your employees and everyone who worked yesterday and their hours? And a copy of yesterday's schedule."

Meadow flew back to the office. The timecards floated in front of her.

"Oh, I never clocked in!" Airie said.

I checked my phone. "Due to your timeline, it would have been 10:45 or so when Airie arrived. Would you like to pencil that in for her?"

"Since you are holding a pencil, if you would," Meadow said. "I don't think any of us will forget this morning."

"Now, do you have any other issues with employees?" Norma asked.

"No, none," Meadow said. That was also a lie.

A knock on the glass front door interrupted my thoughts.

Weyna's husband, Craig's pointed shoes tapped against the glass in the window. By his side was another younger pixie who must be Basilla Columbine, Persimmon's fiancée. The pixies were bundled up for their outdoor work. Their short kilts blew in the breeze over their stained leggings. Their puffy jackets were covered in dirt.

A movement behind the pixies caught my attention. I fought the shiver moving down my spine as Meadow went to let them in.

Two dark figures in long coats, scarves, and fedoras walked westward. I sensed they were undead, perhaps even vampires. They moved too fast to figure out who they were. I put my fingers into my sleeves to warm them and to hide my shaking hands. *Are they heading to my apartment? Don't be stupid!* An old fear crept in my undead heart.

In *Son of Dracula*, 1943, the protagonist, Katherine, is set on fire while asleep in her coffin. I had seen the movie long before I became a vampire, but afterwards, the scene needled my mind during the day and churned with visions of my creator's final death. I often would wake screaming and hide in my or Derrik's closets. Derrik had scolded me for not behaving like a vampire, but fear of the flame had been stronger than fear of a lecture.

I shook the bad memories away and focused on the two pixies who just entered the café.

Craig was a little shorter than his wife. His green skin looked patchy and raw from the cold. His hands were calloused from his work as a landscaper. He removed his cap, exposing his wind-blown silver hair sticking out odd angles.

Basilla had straight golden-blond hair, but her purple skin was ruddied and callous hands of a landscaper. Her face was as still as a mask, but the grinding of her teeth and downcast eyes held back the fear, fury, and sorrow from losing one who was very much beloved from erupting forth. I had seen the expression many times before — even among the vampires. There was so much sadness in the world.

"By the flowers, is it true?" Basilla said.

"Yes, I am sorry to say..." I began.

"Let me see Persimmon. Maybe it's not even her. I want to see Persimmon!" Basilla shouted. She punched a chairback. The sound echoed off all the hard surfaces in the empty coffee house.

I sympathized with her pain though I never had a fiancé or a fiancée myself. I gently opened the hand-carved box. I was glad I had brought the box, silk handkerchief, and flowers. Persimmon looked at rest.

Basilla's no longer spoke, but howled and wept into her fists. "I am going to kill whoever did this. If it's that cat…"

I did not want to hear details about harming an animal. I interrupted with: "I'm very sorry for your loss."

I covered Persimmon's face with the handkerchief, closed the box, and crossed the room as my phone binged again.

Carlos: **Here. Order me the biggest Americano they have.**

Me: **On it.**

I repeated the order. Airie fluttered to the counter to make it.

"You're thinking about coffee at a time like this?" Basilla shouted.

"Madame, I'm sorry for your loss, but my associate and I are normally asleep at this hour. Coffee fuels the brain. Carlos and I need it if we are going to solve the murder."

Basilla swore under her breath as she turned away and audibly wept.

Meadow flitted across the room and sat beside Basilla on the table. She wrapped her arms around her and held her as she wept. There was a certain softness in her eyes as she looked at the broken soul. I couldn't tell if the young pixie was just kind, but my instincts said, she was attracted to Basilla.

Carlos knocked on the window. He had thrown on the same clothing he had been wearing the night before. Not that it mattered. He always looked great. Even under his loose hoodie, his broad shoulders appeared to be hewn from solid granite; his muscles sculpted to perfection. He had been a luchador, before an in-ring accident claimed his wrestling career. Hoping to find a cure, he died after receiving some questionable medical advice from a werewolf shaman. After I gave him a job, he kept his corpse well-preserved with mostly clean living, a low carb diet and the occasional body part from a corpse. Though Persimmon's body was too small to be of much use to Carlos.

Though people often complained of the Seattle Freeze, ingrained politeness of the city made people shake hands with Carlos. Yet in the depths of their heart, they felt icy chronophobia when he set his milky undead gaze upon their face. Everyone knows zombies always win.

Airie went to open the door, a giant Americano floating in front of her.

Carlos raised his cup to let the pixies know he liked it. He made a little growl as he sipped his Americano.

Carlos sat beside me and opened the box and the handkerchief. He nodded slowly. He pulled his pad from his pocket and readied his pen.

"Where did your cats come from?" I asked.

"They were a litter of stray kittens we found over at the park. We brought them to the vet had them cleaned up, spayed, all their shots. But they've never hurt a fly," Weyna said softly.

"All three cats are females then?" I asked.

"Yes. All licensed and legal."

"Now you have a webcam?" I asked.

"Yes."

"Carlos shall watch the footage of last night from close

to open to see if Captain Fluffy McWhiskers is innocent. And if she is guilty, we will take her from this place."

"You can't!" Weyna said. "She's our most popular cat on Instagram!"

Carlos looked at me askance.

"If she killed my Persimmon, I will kill that cat," Basilla suddenly roared from across the room.

Meadow took a few steps away from the rage.

I put my hand up. "Calm down if you please."

"No, that cat has killed before! We know she has," Basilla screamed. "That cat would hurt a fly."

I steadied my gaze at Weyna. "Has Captain or any of the cats hurt anything before?"

"We've found dead bugs, a few mice, but never one of the pixies. They are used to us," Weyna said.

I was pretty sure that was the truth, but I would need more coffee before long.

Chapter 6

Noon

LEAVING THE PIXIES TO THEIR GRIEF, Carlos and I went into the cat lounge and closed the door.

Chocolate Puddin' padded to us and meowed. Carlos scooped her up and scratched her chin. He made a high pitch sound to the cat. Even as she looked him in the eye, Chocolate Puddin' seemed to know that he was a good man and would never hurt her. He sat on the bench and cuddled the friendly little cat. Pirate Jac eyed them from her perch. Captain Fluffy McWhiskers rolled on the floor playing with a felt mouse. I flicked the mouse and Captain dashed after it.

Carlos was a cat lover with three cats of his own. I really didn't know the depth of his cat-related knowledge, but expected to rely upon it today.

We went over the evidence I had collected, my first impressions and I repeated the information I had gathered from the pixies.

Carlos wrote: Any suspects yet?

"All of them." I showed him the photos of the body. "I am sure Persimmon was not killed on the straws. And you know, there are some clues that Captain Fluffy McWhiskers might have done it, but none of the clues make sense. What if someone wanted to set Captain up to take her out of here?"

Carlos's brow creased with his frown. He glanced out the window to the pixies.

He scrawled: Would you have done this if not for me?

"Probably. Wait, what? This job?"

Carlos: Being a detective.

"Sure. Assuming I existed, I think so." I had a similar conversation with Derrik a few times.

Carlos: Because I wouldn't be a detective if not for you.

"Are you saying you want to quit?"

He shook his head.

"Because..."

Carlos put his finger up in the air.

I waited. *What if he didn't want to work with me anymore or come to family dinners or ?* When I felt anxious, it was hard not to chatter. I spent a lot of time alone. I couldn't spend eternity hanging around people who were the same age as I appeared.

Carlos was really my only friend who asked nothing of me. Just being me was enough. Within the coven, I was loved by Agata, Pascaline, Derrik and maybe Jakub and Ryan. The elder vampires got used to having me around. I was pretty much accepted by everyone else as their most profitable business asset four decades running. However, I was also despised as the Shame of the Paper Flower Consortium. The younger vampires were mostly nice to my face. They attempted to hide their dismay of my youthful body, teenage recklessness, and how my brain had never developed beyond a fourteen-year-old girl.

However, they could not hide what they truly dreaded: how I mimicked humanity — even decades after my Rebirth. They feared my way of dress, which allowed me to move unseen through the city. They feared the interactions with werewolves, merfolk, sea serpents and, now, pixies. They feared how I remained ahead of technology and entertainment. As a vampire, I had already accepted I would walk alone.

Though Carlos didn't have many friends as a shade, he once had a real life before he was turned.

He wrote: If one of these kitties hurt that pixie, I'm not letting those pixies hurt her back. She's an animal. If she hurt them, it was instinct. Just as if she had caught a bird.

I sighed in relief.

He continued: Someone is always hurt when we solve a murder, but it won't be an animal.

"Of course, I'd not let someone hurt an innocent animal. We'll take the cat to your house or mine if your cats won't accept her," I said.

Carlos smiled and made a growl in agreement. We bumped fists.

"Do you think the cats will be upset if you need to bring in another cat?"

He shook his head and wrote: I can take her home, if need be.

I was happy that was settled, but I wasn't sure if I was happy that or not that Carlos would take the cat. It had been decades since I last had a pet. Compared to vampires, they died quickly.

"Did you like the coffee?"

He nodded.

"If we solve the crime, we get free coffees for a year and I can use this place for hunting. Don't worry. You'll get your paycheck, of course, and I guess hazard pay for this."

Carlos shook his head. Hazard pay?

"Well, you might get scratched?"

He wrote: Not by this kitty. She's a lover.

"Or a pixie might cast a spell on you. Who knows? Also I looked over the employee records. There is at least one witch who works here. I recognized the name from one of Pascaline's charity mailing lists." I bit my lip and looked around at nothing, at everything.

Carlos: Worried what the coven will say about lack of cash payment?"

I shrugged. "I don't know. Three hundred sixty-five $9 barter payments is probably kind of strange, but I'm helping a small business and a neighbor. The coven will like that."

Carlos flipped the page in his notebook and wrote:

American short hair plus something. Littermates.

Chocolate Puddin': Chocolate/cinnamon torbie with white mitts. Green eyes.

Pirate Jac: Classic black and red torbie with white mitts and blaze. Green eyes.

Captain Fluffy McWhiskers: Dilute blue/cream torbie with white mitts and face, Blue eyes.

"What does torbie mean?" I asked.

Carlos flipped back to the page before and wrote: Tortoiseshell cats with tabby patterns. He pointed out the patterns in Chocolate Puddin's fur.

"When you're ready, hold the cat up," I said. "I'm going

to retake pictures of all their paws again. I tried to do it alone, but it'll be easier with the two of us."

Since Carlos was already holding Chocolate Puddin', I gently separated the fur on her paws and took pictures of all her claws. I sniffed each one. "I don't smell blood."

No. Not on that sweet kitty, Carlos thought - strong enough I could read him.

Pirate Jac was also clean. Then Captain Fluffy McWhiskers. Though she had blood stuck on her leg, there was no blood her claws or between her pads.

Captain Fluffy McWhiskers started to writhe as we examined her. The cat was not injured.

As best as I could with the cat squirming, I scratched the blood out of her fur and collected it into a baggie. I touched it on my tongue.

"Bad news. It's Persimmon's," I said to Carlos. "But that doesn't mean I think Captain did it."

I scraped a credit card over the carpets. There was no blood tracked onto the perches. I ran a piece of tape over each one. All that came up was cat hair.

Carlos wrote: So?

"I think I can be pretty positive Persimmon was not killed in here," I said. "The door to the cat lounge was unlocked when Weyna and Meadow arrived. Captain was out of the lounge, but the other two were inside asleep."

Carlos: Doesn't mean anything. Cats play and sleep on their own schedule. Depending on how long the door was open, they might have come in and out several times.

"Weyna said Captain was an Instagram star. Want to go over the footage?" Norma asked.

He nodded. Greatest job ever.

I left the cat lounge. Carlos petted the cats one more time, made a few sounds to them, and joined me in the retail area.

"Can someone show us the video footage?" I asked.

"Yes. I will," Meadow fluttered towards us. "This way."

We followed Meadow into the office.

As cute as the front of the store and cat lounge was, the back office was painted white walls over the polished concrete floors. I could feel a chilly breeze from the back door. The room had a little of the older building dankness. The west walls were covered with a work schedule, time clock, business license, and posters from the city. One described Seattle worker's rights, the second explained food handlers guidelines, and the third Seattle's recycling/composting/garbage laws. The south wall held a bank of lockers. A large file cabinet and white Formica desk with an old computer on it abutted the north wall. The keyboard looked grubby and stained with sweat and dirt.

Due to her small size, the pixie didn't type. She hit the keys with her whole hand and used magic gestures to move the mouse. She brought up the webcam footage from the night prior.

The camera started at 9:24 and stopped shortly after 10:30 PM.

There's more to this crime than it first appeared. Something happened at 10:30 PM. Something someone didn't want everyone to know about. And no cat could turn off the camera.

"Who has access to this computer?" I asked.

"Everyone, but normally the night shift turns it on when they lock up. Cats enjoy playing at night. We get the best videos after everyone leaves," Meadow said.

"What about footage earlier that day?"

"We don't always run the cameras during the day. Not only does it save energy, but we don't want to have a privacy issue with our clients," Meadow said. "They agree at special events."

Carlos wrote: Possible glitch?

"Anything is possible. The same night that there was a murder? That's a pretty big coincidence," I said."Can we watch footage from the night before?"

Meadow brought it up.

Not wanting Meadow to see our discussion, I texted Carlos: **Check how many nights are missing or if there is missing time during the nights. I'm going to keep talking with the pixies and try to read the cats' minds.**

We bumped fists and went to our respective tasks.

Chapter 7

12:10 PM

THOUGH MY EYELIDS WERE HEAVY, I SAT on the bench in the cat lounge. Chocolate Puddin' mewed, but I picked up Captain Fluffy McWhiskers and petted her with long strokes down her back. Due to the blood found on her leg, I wanted to view her memories first.

"Captain Fluffy McWhiskers, Kitty, Kitty," I said.

When the cat met my eyes, I opened my mind. In some ways, an animal was easier to read than a human because they rarely fought the connection. Moreover, if Captain Fluffy McWhiskers had done the deed, she would feel no shame about it. However, due to the lack of their knowledge of time, the memories weren't organized. Or they were ordered in a way that meant sense to cats, not vampires.

Through Captain Fluffy McWhiskers' eyes, I saw the cat's gray paws batting at Persimmon on the straw. When the pixie didn't get up, the cat made a plaintive merow.

I felt the cat's emotional response: the closest vampire emotion was exasperation. Captain hadn't thought the pixie was dead; she thought Persimmon was sleeping or ignoring her. Captain Fluffy McWhiskers nuzzled her scent upon the pixie. When the pixie still didn't respond, she jumped off the counter and went to the coffee counter.

I tried to open the cat's mind further, to see if she could see who killed the pixie. Though I saw the pixie and human-sized staff, the images were jumbled out of order.

I grew dizzy at Captain Fluffy McWhiskers' remembered spirited dashing across the perches and jumping across the room. I found a memory of Captain Fluffy McWhiskers sniffing at the blue jelly before racing away again.

The sweet smell turned my stomach. I broke the connection before I vomited.

I checked the other two cats' minds. There were no images that made it look like they were the killers or saw the killers. However, Carlos had been right. All three cats had used the open door to their advantage and went exploring the previous night. They hunted a few spiders who dared try to use the café as a home, but not pixies.

I sighed.

Listening to Chocolate Puddin's nonstop purrs, I was beginning to think I might enjoy having someone to cuddle again. I whispered into the cat's ear. "It's too bad you aren't the murderer, if I had a cat, I'd want a cat just like you."

I pressed my cheek to the top of the cat's furry head. I left the cat lounge and went to find Carlos.

He was still in the office and had written a note: Cameras have been turned off every two or three days. These days coincide with small discrepancies in the register or people complaining tip jar was short.

"I understand how they track the register, but how do they track the cash tips?"

He tapped on his pad to a preprinted answer: Don't

know.

Since I spoke out my thoughts in question form all the time, he did not bother to tell me I was asking the wrong person, but I was asking the wrong person and I knew it.

He tapped on: Find anything?

"No. But I am sure none of the cats is the murderer. I couldn't see any of them hurting one of the pixies."

Carlos: Good. You think they are safe?

"For now, but I think they will really be safe when we figure out who did this," I said. "I don't trust Basilla's temper."

Carlos: Me neither.

"Would you examine the pixie's footwear and take prints?"

Carlos: Keep them busy?

"Yeah," I said. "And who knows we might get lucky. I'm going to ask Meadow to call in the vampire-sized staff."

Carlos: Don't you mean shade-sized staff?

Chapter 8

12:20 PM

C ARLOS AND I RETURNED INTO THE MAIN retail area. The five pixies looked up at them from their chair near the Christmas tree. I sensed the immediate rise in the room's tension at our arrival.

Craig sat beside Weyna and held her hand. His face set as if the little pixie was made of stone. Though Meadow was cut from both of her parents in looks, she seemed to take after her father in stoic personality. Basilla and Airie sat on either side of Meadow, not talking.

"Can we take your footprints?" I asked. "And Meadow, please call in your big staff."

"Why?" Meadow lifted off the chair, her wings fluttering violently.

"There is very little evidence that one of the cats acted out of character," I said.

"What about the blood on Captain?" Basilla shouted. Unlike the other pixies, Basilla wasn't fluttering about as she moved, it was as if her heart's sorrow weighed her down. Her tear-stained cheeks had gone the color of a bruise. She was an ugly crier, but the tears looked real.

"Yes, there was blood on Captain, but not on her teeth

or her claws. I am asking you to help Carlos and me figure out who did this. One way to help is by figuring out whose shoes and footprints are around." I raised my hands, palms out. "Perhaps, Persimmon forget something in the café and came back? Maybe a stranger followed her in. Who knows, the cameras were off. Persimmon might even have tried to stop a break-in. The truth is we don't know, we are trying to look for clues."

Basilla jumped up. "Let's get to it then!"

There were a few grumbles, but it was something to do, and people did like to feel useful. Carlos shoe-printed and hand-printed Basilla first since she had jumped up to volunteer. Then he did the rest of the pixies — except Persimmon since I had done so when I cleaned the body.

He went back into the office to file each piece of evidence and compare it to the other footprints I had taken. He also left so I could ask questions. People who weren't afraid to speak to my innocent face clammed up at the hulking silent presence of Carlos.

Basilla grumbled into the Christmas tree, staring into her hot chocolate, which had gone cold. The smudges of fingerprint dust covered her cup.

I didn't want to question the poor woman in her moments of shock and grief. However, if she really wanted to discover who killed Persimmon and why, I must speak to everyone.

"Are you feeling well enough that I might ask you a few questions?" I asked.

Basilla shrugged.

"Is there anyone you know who might see Persimmon

come to harm?"

"No, of course not." Basilla was avoiding eye contact, but I was pretty sure that was the truth.

"And you don't have any enemies?"

"No, no. We were just normal people. We did normal things," Basilla said.

"Do you have children?" I asked.

"We decided marriage first, then children." Basilla choked on the word marriage and she wept out the final words.

I could not read Basilla's mind, but sensed her sorrow and rigorous sense of morality. I learned Basilla lived by a self-imposed strictness. Persimmon was more a free spirit. Basilla did not agree with all of Persimmon's decisions but all of that was over.

"Were you planning to adopt?"

"Yes, but it's expensive," Basilla said sadly. "Even for pixies, $15 an hour only goes so far."

"And that's how much you make over at the Conservatory too?"

"Yes, but I have better benefits which helps."

"And where do you live?"

"In Volunteer Park with my parents, right next to the Pollenjackets," Basilla said.

I wasn't sure what I wanted to ask yet. I learned long ago, I needed to be careful with a person mourning a loved one.

"I noticed Persimmon wasn't wearing in engagement jewelry. Did you exchange a token?"

Basilla eyes narrowed. "Why do you ask? Persimmon

was a kind and loving person, she wouldn't..." *cheat.* Basilla left the last word unsaid.

"I understand," I said. "I am trying to discover if Persimmon might have been robbed? The others told me she loved helping those less fortunate."

Basilla shook her head. Her purple curls spilled out of her hat. "No, she didn't want a token. She wanted to save all our extra money to start our life together and adopting a child."

"Thank you for answering my questions. I'm very sorry for your loss," I said.

Chapter 9

12:30 PM

THE FIRST BIG EMPLOYEE TO ARRIVE WAS the second shift keyholder, a college student named Josh Ali. Their long frizzy hair hung in their face, made more androgynous by good makeup techniques, and the large puffy down coat hung to their knees over ripped jeans.

"We have some bad news," Weyna said. "You should sit down."

Josh did so. They crossed their legs at their ankles and clasped their hands together after they unbuttoned their coat.

"This is hard to say, but Persimmon had an accident last night. We found her this morning," Weyna said.

"Oh God, is she okay?" Josh asked.

"No. She has passed." Meadow glanced back at Basilla.

"Norma is hoping to ask a few questions to help us figure out what happened," Weyna said.

"You aren't a cop, are you?" Josh met my eyes for the first time.

"No, I'm a vampire and private detective." I smiled. "I don't think cops are allowed to dress like me."

"Then it's nice to meet you, luv, and just, FYI my

pronoun is they," they said.

"And you as well. My pronoun is she," I replied. "My associate, Carlos's pronoun is he." The sharing of pronouns was a newer custom for me, but I found it easy enough to remember in Capitol Hill – a historically LGBTQ+ neighborhood.

Josh radiated vitality as they shook my hand. Even though their power hadn't matured, I could see they were a witch. With those spellbinding blue eyes, no doubt, they bewitched all those who fell under their steady gaze. Derrik would say the Master Sculptor had taken His time with Josh.

I had known a few transgender, pangender, two spirit, and agender vampires in the decades of my existence. Every vampire regardless of gender, sexuality, nationality, or religion had been welcomed in the Paper Flower Consortium since its founding in 1855 and most others before that. It became official in all covens after the International Initiation Laws were created in 1921. Witches were pretty open about such things. Though humanity in the western world was becoming more open up about such things again, even living in liberal Seattle, Josh probably had faced several challenges in their life that I didn't understand.

"I've seen vampires slip in and out of the clubs, but I don't know many," Josh said. "Are there any customs I should use, luv?"

"I grew up in Seattle, so I'm pretty casual for a vampire. You can call me by my given name. Other vampires are not so much. And I wouldn't call Carlos 'luv', luv."

The casual use of endearments bothered me a little, but I was also used to it. I wasn't sure if it was his innate manliness or a cultural thing, but it would bother Carlos to be called an endearment, except Bro, Brother, or Dude, unless the person saying it was an elderly woman. (Elderly women could get away with anything with Carlos!)

Though every once in a while, Carlos called her "Dude" — like many west coasters of his generation, he used it in a gender-neutral manner when someone was acting stupid. He sometimes also wrote "Sis" or "Bro" or the Spanish equivalents which were common endearments from his twelve years as a pro wrestler. Since most coven vampires called each other, "Honored Brother, Sister, or Sibling" most of the vampire family assumed I embraced Carlos as one of my honored brothers.

"Are you related to or are you the Joshua Ali who donated to Witch Today last month? My honored sisters helped organize a function for the charity," I asked.

"My father." Josh had a slight twinge of emotion, which they pushed down. *Interesting.* I might push on that topic later, but right now, I was keeping it friendly. I might need Josh to tell me about the other vampire-sized employees.

Josh and I walked into the office where I introduced them to Carlos properly. They put out their hand. I still felt nothing but warmth.

"Nice to meet you, Carlos. Forgive me, but you aren't a vampire, are you?"

Carlos shook their hand then showed them the card in his pocket that read: I am a shade aka a revenant.

Carlos didn't use the word "zombie" unless he wanted to scare people. Thanks to American horror films, zombies had a lot of negative stereotypes. People thought they were

63

irrational monsters who ate human flesh or brains without thought. Carlos liked meat, but he never ate brains. They were slimy.

"Forgive me, you don't speak?"

Carlos's next card read: Crushed Larynx. Body rejected a donated larynx.

I pushed a second chair over for Josh to sit beside Carlos. I sat on a short step ladder.

"A vampire and a shade solve crimes?" Josh asked.

Carlos had a card that read: It's a living.

Josh chuckled then smothered it. "Sorry."

"It's okay. Lots of people laugh when they are nervous. Since you are here, do you mind if we ask you some questions?" I asked.

They squinted a little bit and their heart beat a bit faster as they sat with their knees closely together. "Sure."

"Can I take your coat, it's kind of warm in here."

Josh nodded and removed their coat.

"Which locker is yours?"

"They aren't assigned, but I often use the second one."

I opened the second locker. It was empty. I hung Josh's coat on the hook. I pressed my hands against the pockets. I felt nothing, but a set of keys. *Was a car key stiff enough to impale a pixie?* I sniffed them quickly. Their keys were clean. They didn't smell of anything other than down and Josh-sweat. I handed the keys to Josh.

They thanked me.

"Did anything out of the ordinary happen last night before you closed?" I asked.

"No. It was pretty quiet. I don't remember the exact

number, but the receipts were a little under $300 for the night shift."

"And is that pretty normal for a Wednesday night?"

"Pretty normal." Josh didn't exactly lie, but they were hiding something.

I glanced at Carlos for confirmation. Carlos signaled that his earlier research confirmed $300 was the average.

"And after you closed, what was the rest of your night like for you?" I asked.

"Well, I went to Lola's."

"Did anyone see you?"

"Sure. My partner's a bartender there. Everyone knows me. I had a drink and waited 'til my partner's dinner break. We had dinner together. The bar lets me buy an employee meal. Then I went home and did some studying, but my family was asleep when I got there. I swear I wouldn't have hurt Persimmon."

Since I was sure that Josh would swear that whether they were guilty or innocent, I said in a kind, calming voice: "It's all right, Josh. I'm just trying to put a timeline together. Excuse me, are those the shoes you wore last night to work?"

"What? Yes. Yes, they are," Josh said.

"May we take impressions? We are still working under the assumption; Persimmon was killed by a stranger."

Josh nodded and stood up. "What do I do?"

I wasn't sure why, but Josh seemed more comfortable with Carlos so I brought him the impression supplies.

While Josh stepped heavily on the contact paper, I asked, "Oh, one more question: how do you count up the cash tips?"

"After each shift, we count them up and divide them evenly."

"And that happens how many times a day?"

"Two or three depending on the day."

As Carlos labeled the evidence, I said, "Thank you, Josh."

I heard movement and the pixies speaking louder in the retail area. I led Josh out of the back office to discover what was happening.

Two young college-age people, a Black woman and a White man, were walking down the street toward the café. Their breath forming clouds in the cold air.

"Who are they?" I asked.

"Zoe Wilson and Jaimie Hall," Josh said.

While they were still outside, I asked, "Are they an item?"

Josh replied, "Just roommates."

Chapter 10

1:00 pm

I WATCHED JAIMIE TAKE A FEW LONG STEPS in front of Zoe and hold the door open for her. That might mean romantic entanglement, or it might mean nothing more than he was taught that's what a gentleman does. Or just because his legs were a little longer.

A pretty college student who had dyed her long box braids into an umbra effect of blue to pink, Zoe rubbed her gloved hands together as if the sudden warmth of the café made her fingers sting. "What's going on? Persimmon was in some sort of accident?"

I waited to see who would respond, but wondered, *how long that umbra effect took in the salon chair, or did Zoe do it herself?* I didn't ask because I didn't want to be seen as a non-professional, but it was an excellent dye effect.

Jaimie wore his hair in what mostly was his natural color. His light brown hair held hints of red, but the grainy stubble on his face was auburn. Jaimie was close to his adult height, but his shoulders were still narrow. He appeared a few years younger than Zoe and Josh, probably a freshman or sophomore. He was also a bit more nervous as he watched me study him. He unzipped his jacket and took it off. His pounding heart and sweat irritated my bloodlust. I ignored it.

I wished I could read his mind. I needed another cappuccino for sure. *How many was that?* I had no idea. *I better wait.*

"Weyna asked me to figure out what happened. Now I'm a private detective, not a cop. I am just here to solve the mystery," I said.

"And if you do figure it out?" Zoe said.

"I get free coffee for a year and a place to hang out."

"I meant what happens to us?"

I used my vampire street-cred to my advantage. "I am a licensed PI and a vampire. One thing Hollywood got right about us, is we are obsessive puzzle solvers."

"Josh told me you're roommates?"

Zoe didn't say anything.

Jaimie opened his mouth, but clamped it shut, following Zoe's lead.

Weyna started crying again. "You must answer her questions. I asked her to be here. No one else helps the pixies."

"You invited a vampire inside?" Jaimie said. "Weyna, you are never supposed to invite a vampire inside, it makes them invincible."

"Good grief," I muttered.

"I'm not talking to you without my lawyer." Zoe pressed her lips closed.

I knew bluster when I heard it. However, I also knew if I were in Zoe's situation, I would absolutely call Derrik so he might act as my attorney.

"Fine with me. Call them, please."

Zoe's lips trembled.

"This is not a court of law. I'm not a cop. The only thing that might happen is someone loses their job. And honestly, you know as well as I do that having a pixie boss means your next boss isn't going to know or care."

Zoe glared for a moment, but I didn't drop my gaze.

"Alright, I'll answer your questions." Zoe's words were clipped at the consonants. I could feel a low anger or perhaps expectation that I planned to trick them someway.

I figured I needed to question around the topic to warm up Zoe. "Do you believe Captain or one of the other cats hurt Persimmon?"

"What, the cats?" Zoe's eye's widened.

"The cats."

"You think..." Zoe trailed off.

"If I don't prove that Captain did not kill Persimmon, Basilla is going to kill her. And it doesn't sound like just put her to sleep either."

"But the cats are super gentle. I've never seen them swipe at the pixies," Jaimie said.

"Would you agree with that?" I asked.

Zoe's eyes softened towards Weyna. "Yes," she said a little bit crispy.

"And you are roommates?" I tried again.

"Yes," Jaimie said.

"Here in the neighborhood?"

"A little higher on the hill."

That wasn't surprising; the farther from downtown rents got a little cheaper. "And my understanding is that you are not lovers, just share the apartment."

Zoe pulled at her long tunic-style shirt. "Yes."

"When was the last time you saw each other last night?"

"After I got home, Zoe was watching some stupid reality show and studying in the living room. We said hey. I went into the kitchen, made some noodles, and then into my room. Studied for awhile, went to sleep."

"So you're both still in school?"

"Yes. I'm getting my master's in business," Zoe said.

"What are you studying, Jaimie?"

"Computer Science," he said softly.

They were interrupted by fourth and final employee, Hannah Cameron. She ran into the café, her ivory cheeks made red from the cold, her long blond hair in a loose ponytail.

"What happened?" Hannah's breath had a slight wheeze. She must have jogged over here. Her expression lacked guile, but I wondered if it was practiced. I felt the temptation of stopping the pulse under her delicate white throat.

The café seemed quite full with the minds of five pixies, one very young witch not yet in their powers, and three humans. Their fast, worried thoughts overwhelmed my mind. So much was meaningless noise. I got a strong sense of the word: *Keys.* That could mean anything. Stupid mind-reading ability wasn't always accurate especially when I was sleepy.

"Meadow, I need another cappuccino," I said. I didn't really want coffee, I wanted blood, but coffee would have to do.

Jaimie crossed his arms in front of him. "Aren't you a little young to be drinking cappuccino?"

I glimpsed just enough in his mind that Jaimie was a fan of the worst kind of freaking vampire novels. Which meant a too-young vampire standing in front of him creeped him out. The others were a little interested in meeting a vampire and a shade, but they were a lot less curious about me. They feared I might suspect they were murderers.

"It's not like it's going to stunt my growth," I said.

"I just meant, wouldn't you rather have a granita or something?" Jaimie asked.

"Uh, it's freezing out there. A few degrees lower and it would be snowing."

"Are you still in school?" Jaimie asked.

"I graduated in 1958."

"High school?" Jaimie asked.

Though I didn't like to be off-track, I reckoned I needed to share a bit about myself and then bring the conversation back to Persimmon's murder. "No, U'dub. When I was as young as this form appears, I had a private tutor until I went to U'dub. The vampires who raised me did not trust my bloodlust around other teenagers with good reason."

"The vampires..." Jaimie trailed off.

"Good grief, Jaimie," Zoe cried. She knew the kind of books her roommate read.

"Oh, sorry." Jaimie blushed.

"It's okay, Jaimie, I get your question a lot. I was created by a vampire whose child had died in a war. I was his daughter. Nothing more. And when he couldn't take care of me, his creator raised me."

I smiled to allow Jaimie to see a bit of fang. As expected, he was excited because he was meeting a real vampire and repulsed by my outer shell. It's why I disguised myself when I went to clubs. "My bloodline progenitor also only ever saw me as a girl and he is a Victorian prude." That wasn't exactly true. I was aware Derrik was not a prude, but he could be prudish by today's standards.

Hannah, Josh, and Zoe were also relieved.

The pixies seemed annoyed, because to their eyes, they didn't see much of a difference between me, Carlos, and the other young people in the room.

Bringing the conversation closer to the point, I asked, "Hannah, do you go to school too?"

Hannah nodded. "Yes, I'm studying early childhood education." I sensed that was true. Time to ask more leading questions.

"How do you all feel about working here?"

"I love working here," Zoe said. "Everyone is lovely to us. No one comes into a pixie and cat café to be in a bad mood. Even if they do, they leave happy."

"I enjoy it too," Jaimie said. "Zoe helped me get this job. I used to work at a chain coffee house; people are nicer here. Not as much as in a rush."

So Jaimie followed Zoe's lead in a lot of things. *Interesting*.

"I like working here too," Hannah said. Suddenly I got a little twinge Hannah lied. "With tips, we make decent enough money," she said. "And nearly everyone tips." Truth.

"Do you two live alone?" I asked Hannah and Josh.

"I live with a roommate," Hannah said.

"I still live with my parents," Josh said.

"How well did you know Persimmon?"

"We worked with her during the shift change five days a week, but that's only a few hours. I'd say she was a happy person. She loved her fiancée," Hannah said.

"Yes, she always spoke of you with such adoration," Jaimie said softly to Basilla who sat with Meadow in the corner.

"And who are the keyholders?" I asked.

"Josh, Weyna, and Meadow," Zoe said.

Airie brought me another cappuccino. I downed the shot in one gulp. The caffeine hit my system and smoothed the darting whispers spinning all around me.

Thank god for coffee.

"Do you know what this is?" I showed the two young women the bag.

"It looks like some melted jellies."

"I didn't see any jellies on the counter."

"We don't do boba or jellies. Too much competition with the Boba Tea places," Meadow said.

"Are those the shoes you wore last night to work," I asked the employees.

"Yes."

"And can we get impressions of them?"

Jaimie said, "Yes."

Hannah and Zoe both declined to cooperate.

"She's a vampire. She will know if you are lying. So we might as well cooperate," Jaimie said.

"It's an invasion of my privacy," Zoe said. "Plus, a hundred people must have walked over this floor. It doesn't mean anything."

Hannah said nothing.

Zoe isn't management or a keyholder, but she's a natural leader. How many of the employees looked to Zoe for guidance?

I wished I had met Zoe under better circumstances.

Chapter 11

1:15 PM

I PRETENDED I COULDN'T HEAR JAIMIE AND Zoe whispering in the corner, by the Christmas Tree. Airie, Hannah, and Josh were making drinks and plating up pastries with Weyna's permission.

"Look, I'm not like you. I don't care if she's a vampire," Zoe said to Jaimie. Though her voice was low, not above a whisper, the anger elevated her tone and sharpened her enunciation. "There's no reason to cooperate with her."

"Weyna said to cooperate," he replied.

God, Jaimie is young, I thought.

"Well, I don't trust she isn't ultimately going to call the cops," Zoe said.

I couldn't fault Zoe for her attitude. *With stories about ICE ignoring warrants and arresting innocent people and people of color being shot by the cops, Zoe might be right not to cooperate.* "As far as the cops are concerned, no crime has been committed — or if it has been it's the stealing," Jaimie said, rubbing his hands over his arms.

"Says her," Zoe stopped talking as Hannah and Josh drew near.

The two thanked Airie, Hannah and Josh who brought

over some breakfast. Once they were seated, Weyna fluttered around the four and begged them to cooperate.

Frowning, Meadow flitted towards the group, stopped, and backed off.

"You have something to say?" I asked. I might not be able to read pixie's the way I could read witches and humans, but vampires — especially those raised by an attorney — tended to be excellent at directing conversations. Meadow was ready to talk.

"I know what those damn kids are whispering," Meadow said.

"You do?"

"That I'm a crap boss and stole from the tip jar."

Seeing the crack in Meadow's business-like façade, I pressed for information while slowing backing away to separate Meadow from the others. "What makes you say that?"

Meadow followed. "I'm the one that tries to make them work. I haven't taken a paycheck in a month. Not that they would care. It was probably one of those kids. They sit around. When I'm not here, they give extras to friends."

"If more supervision is needed, why do you and your mother work together?" I asked and sat down at a table near the shaded window.

Meadow sighed. "We don't. Or I should say, we do work together a few times a week. Normally, she opens, then I come in a few hours later, so there are at least three pixies on hand during our busiest hours. Today was our management meeting."

"What does that entail?"

"Going over the sales, budget and scheduling, supply. We've been trying to get better at figuring out which desserts sell and trying to figure out where the losses have been coming from."

"Do you like running this business with your mom?"

"Yes," Meadow made a slight pause. "This is the best thing we did together." *A lie.*

"There's been no problems?"

"Not really."

I pressed. "Other than the business growing slower than you'd like, of course?"

Meadow sighed again. "I love working with my mom, but she's a little too inconsistent."

"How so?"

"When we first opened, she made Zoe give samples to everyone on the street, including people who would never be customers."

Meadow meant the homeless people who no doubt surrounded the poor girl trying to get a morsel of the treat. While most homeless would have been kind to her, not all would. There were jerks in every level of society.

"It's like she forgot the Seattle she knew as a girl has been gone for decades. Seattle's not a small city anymore, but she never says no. A homeless person comes in and tells her a sob story and she makes them a coffee."

"She said no to Persimmon's long vacation," I said.

"And Persimmon knew that she didn't mean it, which is why she laughed."

"Well, Washington is an at-will state. Everyone is hiring. Do you have any less-that-friendly competition with the other cafés?"

"No. We got in a tiff once about the apartment building across the street A-board sign blocking our door, but they moved it after we..."

"You what?"

"We complained, but they didn't do anything. So we sent Josh over to complain. It's hard to say anything to a clean-cut, good-looking kid like them."

"Tell me about your employees."

"Persimmon, Airie, and I all went to school together so once I was hiring I was happy to hire my friends. That might have been a mistake. Airie enjoys the work well enough, but she sometimes felt outshone by Persimmon. She's a little competitive for a service job, but she likes working inside.

"As for the big people, Josh and Zoe have worked for us the longest. Both of them over a year. Zoe is incredibly reliable."

"I got that sense from her too."

"Josh is a little less diligent, but they are a hard worker. They are only the keyholder because of the hours they are willing to work."

"And the others?"

"Jaimie is good at following direction and eager to please. Hannah is routinely five-minutes late to everything, but once she is here, she is great on the floor and a terrific barista. Always happy."

"The cats love all of them. That's part of our interview process, if Chocolate Puddin' doesn't come up to someone as soon as they enter the cat lounge they are not hired. We trust every single one of them."

"What do you think happened?"

"Well, I think someone from the outside followed Persimmon last night."

I nodded, but during other jobs, I had heard several suspects put suspicion on a homeless person or some random drunk guy. From what I had seen, most homeless folks were just struggling to get by. Tech companies created jobs, but also drove up the rents. Wages had not kept up with the cost of living in the City of Seattle and King county. While Seattle was a big city and random murders had happened, most murders were done by people the victim knew. *More significantly, if it was some rando, there would be no reason to set up the cats.*

"But if Persimmon didn't have a key, how did she get in?" I asked, hoping Meadow would let some information on pixie magic escape.

"That part I don't know," Meadow said. "It doesn't make sense that she was here."

"Can pixies do unlocking spells?"

"Some can, but I doubt Persimmon could. Maybe I'm wrong. Maybe she could unlock the door. She really just did glamours, like the rest of us."

"And what were you doing last night?" I asked.

"The usual. I had dinner with my parents. That would have been about eight. Then I went to my room and watched baking shows until bed."

"Best type of shows there is," I said.

"Sometimes I get ideas for flavors for drinks," Meadow said. "And it helps to figure out which of Anna's desserts are good ideas and which are just a little too chef-y for our customers. Not that any of them taste bad, but some of the more unique flavors don't sell."

Airie flew over. "You might want to figure out whatever you are figuring out faster, because the kids probably won't stay much longer."

I looked up at the pixie, flying above my head. "Meadow, can you try to get everyone to stay, just for a little while longer. Call it a study session or something."

Before I went to get Carlos who would scare the college kids into staying, I asked Airie, "What were you doing last night?"

"You can't pin this on me!" She was already in a tizzy.

"I am not trying to pin it on anyone. I am just trying to figure out where everyone was," I said.

"I was home, alone, watching Netflix. I live alone, how is that a crime?"

"It isn't. What did you watch?"

"A few horror movies," Airie said.

"Good." I needed to make this fast and direct. "Tell me who do you think has been swiping money out of the tip jar?"

"One of those freaking big people."

"Why?"

"Because they don't care. This job is just a stepping-stone for them. I want to work here." She paused and added, "I might not like every minute of my job or even everyone I work with, but I like the job."

I thought that was a weird thing to add, but this was a cushy job. Coffee, hot chocolates, pastries, cats, and working with one (or possibly two) of her school chums. Why would Airie kill Persimmon? With everything the pixies had told me, I could see no reason.

Chapter 12

1:30 PM

I CIRCLED THE COFFEE BAR. I WANTED TO see how different it looked now that a few coffees had been made. I sensed Jaimie's blue eyes a-flicker with curiosity and interest as he watched my movements. He followed me with a quiet grace and a slightly confused expression. For a young man of the modern era, he had great posture.

"What are you thinking about?" I asked.

Jaimie scratched his stubble-covered chin. "It may be nothing, but I remember washing these dishes and setting up for the morning crew and something looks wrong. I just don't know what."

"Can you think about washing the dishes? I can read your memory. If you go through it step by step, we might figure out what it is," I said. Focusing on the young man, I slipped my mind over his. He accepted my will overcoming his without fight, which was good. If he freaked out, it might feel as if insects were crawling all over his brain and I was likely to lose the connection.

He pointed at the three sink basins and drying rack.

"We use a standard three sink system. We don't use the

basins for anything but washing. It helps keep dishwashing efficient as do our cup sizes, and we only do small plates."

"How often is it refilled?"

"Every four hours. You see this checklist."

On a laminated paper with an attached dry erase pen was a simple checklist marked with his initials during his shirt and Hannah's during hers. Beside it was a shelf with commercial dish soap, pH test kit and sanitizer tablets and a hook with a scrub brush.

"Since we just do sweets, I don't normally scrape too much food into the compost which sits here, but the compost in this bin and trash goes in there. Then I wash in the first basin."

"I know this sounds silly, but tell me about the wash basin, every step," I said.

"I fill the first basin with hot, soapy water for washing. I use this scrub brush." He pointed at the brush on the hook.

"How often is it cleaned?" I asked.

In his head, I witnessed his actions followed his spoken directions. For a young man he was a reliable employee. He always did as Weyna, Meadow, or Josh asked of him.

Jaimie kept talking. "Whenever it gets cold or dirty — it almost always gets cold first. Then this is the rinse basin, and this is the sanitizer basin. The dishes soak here for about a minute and set on the rack to air-dry."

He stared at the dish rack. Something was missing. I tried to see his memory from last night -his last look at the dishes. There was eight small plates, ten demitasse cups and saucers, twelve sixteen-ounce mugs, eight forks, three long-handled barista spoons.

In the dry rack, there were four small plates, nine demitasse cups, seven sixteen-ounce mugs, eight forks, and a long-handled barista spoon.

There was another barista spoon in the sink. Where was the third?

A barista spoon is missing! I pressed my thumb on the handle. It was stiff and sharp enough if I applied enough force, I might be able to draw blood. On a pixie, it would be a dangerous weapon.

Trying not to get excited that I might have discovered the murder weapon, I glanced on the floor to see if it had fallen.

"And after you are done with the dishes, each one is filled with hot water to rinse them?" I asked.

"Yes," Josh said behind them. I saw their tell. For the first time, Josh lied.

Jaimie's eyes got wide and he looked to the floor. He knew Josh had lied to me.

I slipped the bag out of my pocket.

"Do you know what this is?"

Josh looked at it. "No."

Another lie.

"Jaimie, you look like you want to say something," I said.

"Well, I can't be sure, but it looks like melted jellies. You know the kind Boba Tea places, but in their drinks."

"Meadow said you don't carry jellies like this?"

"No, but Persimmon loved them. She sucked on them throughout her shift," Jaimie said.

I needed to get Josh in the back with Carlos. He'd get

the truth fast enough. Or perhaps, I should question them alone.

However, that took time that I did not have.

"Josh Ali." I peered into their eyes. They tried to drop my gaze. "Good grief. You are lying to me when you've nothing to lie about," I wondered if the young person would be fooled by such a ploy.

"I'm not lying." An image rose to Josh's mind.

It worked! I learned they spent more time doing homework in the back than helping Persimmon and Jaimie in the front of the house.

"Jaimie is easier to read than you," I lied. "Sorry, but the boy's an innocent, and vampires can always read an innocent mind. So, is there something you want to tell me? We can go to the cat lounge."

"I'll tell you, but don't tell Weyna."

"Let's go into the cat lounge."

I grabbed a few napkins off the condiment stand. I knew they would need a tissue.

They opened the door for me. Once it closed behind them, they said, "Look, I've already gotten two warnings and I really need this job. Persimmon said she'd get me fired."

So Josh was worried about losing their pretty cushy coffee-house job, but that wasn't worth killing someone over, was it? Coffee houses were on every block in Capitol Hill. They were all hiring as were other service-based jobs. But not all jobs had cats as loving as Chocolate Puddin' who immediately jumped onto Josh's arms and purred. Captain and Pirate banged them with their heads. The cats obviously loved Josh.

"I knocked that smug little pixie's jellies onto the ground, but I swear I wouldn't have killed her," Josh whispered.

"I know you didn't." I watched how they responded now that I knew their tell. I was now 99% sure they were not the murderer.

"You do?"

"Yes, but I also know when people are lying to me — and I need the truth. I'm trying to figure out what happened last night until this morning."

Josh rambled about how they are struggling in school. Their family has been supportive about being agender, but they — especially their father — won't understand if they flunk out.

"You're putting a lot of this on yourself. May I hold your hand?" I asked.

"You're not disgusted by me?" They wiped their sleeve on their nose. "I took a pixie's candy away. I swiped at someone small."

I handed them a napkin and then took their free hand. "People make mistakes. Did you hurt her?"

"No, but I knocked the candy straight out of her hands."

Again truth.

Wiping their eyes, Josh said, "It's just so hard. My parents don't even charge me rent, but I pay for the rest of my expenses. I don't know how the others make do. My dad worked his way through college and expects me to do the same, but sometimes I feel too weak to do it."

"Are you safe?" I asked.

Josh's eyes blinked as they tried to focus on her. "Safe?"

"My vampire dad was, uh, strict," I said, thinking of Bill again and wishing I had not. "As I said, I ended up living with my vampire grandpa." That was the nicest version of the facts.

"No, nothing like that. I just feel as if I constantly let the family — especially my dad — down. I mean you knew my father's name and our address which is why you asked when I arrived. And you're a vampire — and not just any vampire — but Norma of Norma's Cleaning Service. You're practically a household name in the community. No one knows me."

"You're twenty-one. No one knew me either when in my twenty-first year of existence. I was still at U'dub too and existing with my vampire grandpa." I paused, not sure if this was a sharing moment or a listening moment.

Josh didn't respond.

I went on, "And I struggled, not like you with gender, but I wrestled to figure out who I was supposed to be as a vampire, growing up, with schoolwork and even who I dated. I admit I was lucky, my vampire dad and his creator were openly bisexual in a time the rest of the world wasn't, but I was pretty freaked out about my sexuality."

"You're bisexual?"

"Yes, but between the Catholic guilt and being a vampire, even my most heteronormative thoughts freaked me out a little bit. Let's just say the 1950's was a weird time for me."

Josh chuckled slightly. They really did tend to laugh during times of stress.

"You will find your own way. I did," I said.

Josh nodded.

I sensed Josh's corpuscles ask for connection. "Do you need a hug?"

"You won't bite me?"

"No. I only bite those who want me to bite them. Besides, I'm so jacked up on coffee, I'd be buzzing the rest of the day if I added blood to the mix."

Josh hugged me a little too hard, but they had wanted a hug. Chocolate Puddin' meowed a complaint at the sudden movement and shifted herself between us to get more comfortable.

This close and alone in the cat lounge, that 99% became 100%. Josh was not the killer.

But Jaimie looked up to Josh. Would Jaimie have killed for Josh? Maybe not on purpose, but in a moment of passion?

Once Josh released me, I asked, "So Jaimie's been covering for you."

"Yeah, but Jaimie was willing."

"Are you covering for him?"

"No. I mean there is nothing to cover for. Freshman classwork isn't that hard for a kid like Jaimie."

"But Persimmon wasn't willing to cover for you?"

Josh sat up straighter. "Persimmon complained to Weyna about it. She said it wasn't fair for me to be studying when there was work to be done. She said she'd get me fired."

"How did Weyna respond?"

"The first time Weyna told me that I was a trusted employee and I should not betray that trust. The second time she said that she was losing patience with me."

"It'll be okay, Josh."

"But it's not okay. The others are my friends, I can't believe any of them would do it. We don't know Basilla," Josh said. "But she has a temper."

"I have seen her temper, but I don't know her either."

"Craig seems like a supportive spouse, but what if he wants to close the cat café," Josh whispered.

"Why would you think that?"

"I don't know because sometimes Meadow is annoyed with her mom? Maybe he's tired of the bickering."

"Perhaps, but it does no good pointing fingers until I know something and can prove it, but I promise, I will figure it out and in someway, justice will be served. But I need your help."

"What can I do?"

"Just make sure Zoe, Hannah, and Jaimie don't leave until I do. Not because I suspect them, but because I need time to figure out what happened," I said. "I have no authority over humans or witches, but you are a natural leader. I've seen how Hannah and Jaimie look up to you."

"I'll do my best." Josh smiled.

Chapter 13

2:00 PM

I NOTICED ZOE SCRAPING SOMETHING OFF her shoe with a straw.

"What's wrong?" I asked.

"Damn it, I stepped in gum or something."

Hannah's pulse rose as I approached. Zoe's did not.

"Let me help you." I said. "Wouldn't want to track it around?"

I pulled it off and collected the sample. It was not the same gum that I found earlier. I dropped a bit of fingerprint powder on the floor, hoping the ruse would work.

I was too tired to gather deep thoughts from the young woman's intellect. Zoe had too much of a strong will, but she was a human with an open mind. At first glance, Zoe seemed to have a strong sense of reliability. According to her timecard, she was punctual and dependable. According to Meadow, she had not taken a sick day in months.

She was open enough to see pixies and accept a job from them. Meeting a vampire didn't faze Zoe, only the thought that I had some sort of authority. Since arguing about authority was a waste of time, I didn't try to convince her otherwise.

Her steadfastness might be why Jaimie tended to follow her lead or it might be that she was a few years older. Sitting across from her, I could sense her determined character.

Hannah seemed more lackadaisical though also more affable. I sensed her eagerness to help solve the mystery, but something preoccupied her.

"What do you think happened?" I asked. "I've heard stories of family bickering and of possible random attack."

Zoe still didn't say anything.

I tried a different tact. "I've heard a rumor that money might have gone missing out of the register or tip jar."

Zoe didn't speak.

"We didn't do it," Hannah said quickly.

"Do you know who did?" I asked.

"No," Hannah said.

"No, I don't either," Zoe said.

"Well, if it was anyone it was Meadow," Hannah said.

"Why do you say that?"

"She's always in need of money. If the bookkeeping was better run, the cat café would be fine. We aren't bringing in the kind of customers like a chain shop, but we are often busy," Hannah said. "Or who knows, maybe, it was Persimmon and Meadow caught her."

Its circling around to the tip jar again. Interesting.

"Someone has been stealing money." I ensured I met the eyes of both women.

"Not a lot," Hannah said.

"What do you mean?"

"She means it's not enough to be noticed, just enough to be off. Jaimie's registers are always accurate, so are mine, but then we end up off. And we are the ones who get snapped at," Zoe said.

"So you think it is Meadow too," I whispered in what I hoped sounding like a conspiring tone.

"No. I don't know," Zoe said. "But the company isn't making expenses and sometimes money is missing during different shifts. It could only be one of the managers, but you didn't hear that from me."

"Thank you for talking to me."

Zoe muttered a profanity under her breath. I had been despised for so long, I refused the offense. Zoe did not like to feel like she was not in control, but she wasn't a murderer.

"Vampires have excellent hearing," I said. "If you are going to talk about me, can you please go in the other room."

Hannah and Zoe both had the decency to blush and mutter sorry, before they left. And I smiled at the impressions left on the floor.

I texted Carlos: **I just got a boot impression from Zoe and Hannah. I need supplies.**

Chapter 14

2:07 PM

AFTER I COLLECTED THE BOOTPRINTS from the floor, I lifted for prints at the window in the bathrooms. I knew that even if Josh and Jaimie did, Hannah and Zoe would not give up their fingerprints. There was no point in arguing with them about it.

The sun had shifted, so the pixies were able to open the window shades. It made the café less gloomy. My phone rang. Agata.

"Hello, Bunica."

"So, Norma, my love, I'm looking at these photos. While your images show her on the straw, I don't see how that could happen. A straw might, at best, scratch some of the delicate wing flesh, but even that is questionable.

"According to my anatomy book, there is no way could it rip through the ribcage and sternum. My best guess is Persimmon was stabbed by something else. Something rigid and then planted on the straw."

"Thanks, Bunica. That's what I was thinking too."

"Will we be seeing you at services?"

I rolled my eyes. *Good grief.* "Yes, Bunica, I'm staying with Derrik all weekend."

"Good. I'll ask Kuma if he is willing to replenish you."

I wanted to tell Agata that wasn't necessary, but Agata did not believe cow's blood was good enough nourishment for the Sabbath. Kuma was generally willing to replenish me because I was the progeny of his own personal goddess.

"Unless you are bringing someone?" Agata said with a note of hope in her voice.

I thought of Jaimie. I might take a little nibble out of him. "No. I'm still single."

"Well, that's too bad."

"I did meet a young man, but he's only eighteen and has some rather romantic ideas about being a vampire."

"And if he came in as your thrall, he'd want to be changed at twenty-five?"

"Yes, I think so."

Agata sighed. "Such people never make good thralls. Try to find a young man who wants to worship you as a goddess."

That was easy for Agata. She was thirty-two when she was transformed and a great lady, the wife of a knight. Her body bore the marks of life. Her accent was from Europe. No one wanted a goddess who was stuck at fourteen and born in America. "Yes, I will. See you this weekend."

I hung up the phone and paced. I tried to parse the information into facts and conjecture.

Last night, Josh and Persimmon quarreled about Josh spending time in the back. Josh knocked some jellies onto the floor and went to the back to study. Josh, Jaimie, and Persimmon closed the café normally. The cameras confirmed, they left a few minutes after nine-thirty. Josh set the alarm and locked the door.

The camera was stopped.

At some point, Persimmon came back. Or did she come back earlier and turn off the camera? Obviously, someone else did too. Or perhaps followed her in. At some point, Persimmon was accidentally or purposefully killed then impaled on a straw.

"What am I missing?"

I picked up a clean straw. I pressed my finger onto the end and applied pressure. It cracked. My fingers was not even scratched.

I took another straw and slammed the palm of my bare hand into it. It also cracked in half. If a straw couldn't scratch her flesh, how did it break through Persimmon's ribs? Through her clothing? But I was a vampire.

"Carlos, can I check something?"

He ambled over. I explained my experiment.

Carlos wrote: Get a pastry. Saw this on Youtube.

"Can I have a few pastries for an experiment?" I asked the pixies.

"Of course, hun," Weyna said. "What kind will you like?"

"Something crusty. Does anything have nuts in it?" I wondered if nuts broke as pixie bones did.

"We have mini pies for the season. Pecan," Meadow said.

Looking at the pastry case, I said, "Okay. Can I have a pecan pie and one of those chocolate croissants and one of those jam-filled croissants?"

"Sure. Do you want them heated?"

"No."

I brought the plate back to Carlos.

With his thumb plugging the hole, Carlos plunged the straw into the pastry. The first straw ripped through the jam and chocolate croissants. It stopped briefly in the pecan pie as it got caught on a nut, but aiming with force, the second straw went right through the pastry.

"So the straw could have been the murder weapon," I whispered. "But if so, where did the missing body parts go? Not to mention the missing spoon?"

Carlos: Don't know. Just didn't want you to get off track. I can always check the dumpsters if you want.

I pursed my lips and called out: "When is garbage collected?"

"Thursdays. Normally in the morning."

Carlos dashed out the back door.

He came back shaking his head.

"Empty?" I asked.

He nodded.

"So, we have two reasons it couldn't be a cat. If the straw were the murder weapon, then the murderer would need a thumb. And a cat wouldn't know when the garbage was collected. Want another coffee?"

He nodded.

I returned to the retail area. "Can someone make me another cappuccino and Carlos another Americano?"

Outside, a man stopped at the window and peered inside. Looking at the seemingly familiar frame, my stomach dropped. I felt as if every blood cell in my body had become a little pebbles tearing through my circulatory system and striking my heart. *I knew you weren't dead. You can't die. No, it's still daylight. Even if Bill existed, he wouldn't be walking around out there.*

I shook my head and looked up again. Bill or Bill's doppelganger was walking away. I ran to the door. Another man, shorter than the first, joined Bill's doppelganger. They both had dark curly hair, which stuck out of fedoras. The feeling of ancient undeath swept over me again. She wanted to climb my bloodline and check the ancients who existed there. But I had a job to do.

I tried to calm herself with a thought. *Even ancient vampires don't often walk in the daylight...*

I am walking in the daylight.

So why couldn't they?

Carlos made a growling sound behind me.

"I thought I saw Bill," I whispered. "But I was talking to Josh, and they have personal issues with their dad. Maybe, it's just my own garbage rising up."

In my existence as a vampire, I would be fine for months — well weeks — at a time. Then I would sense Bill was still in the world though he had been executed.

Carlos clenched his fist then scribbled a message. If somehow Bill came back, I'd never let him hurt you again.

He passed me another piece of paper. Or Derrik. Or anyone in your fam.

I smiled. I appreciated he was trying to let me keep my pride.

I never told Carlos precisely what happened, but Carlos occasionally slept on my couch when the nights went long. He had been Derrik's guest for family Sundays. My dayterrors were not exactly quiet or clean. He heard me scream and had seen sweaty, bloodstained clothing.

"I probably just imagined him. I really need sleep," I said.

Carlos: Want to grab fifteen minutes on the couch? I'm almost done with matching the prints.

"Yeah. Tell them, I'm meditating on the evidence or something."

Carlos: Got it.

Chapter 15

2:21 PM

I LAID DOWN ON THE COUCH IN THE OFFICE. It smelled of old coffee and sugar, but I felt safe enough with Carlos nearby to sleep. Though a nap wouldn't help nearly as the sleep of the dead. However, I doubted I would even get that. My heartbeat pounded in my ears. I had way too much caffeine. With my eyes closed, I went over the evidence.

Persimmon wanted to get married and looking to adopt a child. Basilla in mourning. I believe she is innocent.

Almost no blood splatter, but Captain had blood in her fur.

Agata believes most likely killed and then impaled. Though straws can most likely go through pixie flesh, not sure about the bone. No matter what the weapon, I don't believe she was killed on the condiment counter.

Café not doing well financially. . Craig has no reason. Meadow and Weyna have money problems

Airie...

Josh...

Jaimie...

Zoe...

Hannah...

Does anyone working here not have money problems?

Receipts and register tallies don't always match.

The register. How can I prove that? The tip jar. The tip jar was still full when I came in.

Too soon, I sensed Jaimie's heartbeat enter the room. Sigh.

I forced open my raw eyes and looked up at him. "Yes?"

"I didn't want to interrupt your meditation, but I need to ask you a question? I will hate myself forever if I don't," Jaimie said.

"Sure." I sat up, swung my legs to the floor, and rubbed my eyes.

He plopped down beside me. "Do you think the coven would accept me? I told you about washing dishes and the truth about the jellies."

"Accept you as what?"

"A vampire, of course," Jaimie said.

"You're nineteen?"

"Almost." Jaimie started jittering his leg.

"Almost?" I suddenly was overcome by the urge to have another friend. He was only four years older than I was when I died. I might have a young friend, young like me. Jaimie might like to kiss me without a disguise. We were close enough in apparent age; no one would look twice.

I shook the thought away. It would be death for both of us. Derrik and Pascaline and all who loved me would mourn and then forget me. Jaimie would be forgotten immediately.

There was no chance of a friendship or love for me. There never would be. To give Jaimie what he wanted would kill him. I pushed the old yearning away and met his eyes.

"The coven has a standard three-year initiation program. If you wish to be a vampire, you may contact Lady Pascaline at the Paper Flower Consortium. You would have to wait six years. Since 1921, international law requires all vampires to be changed after their twenty-fifth birthday."

"You weren't twenty-five," Jaimie said.

"The man who made me was tied to a roof to await the sunrise. I almost ended up beside him," I said a half-truth to ensure Jaimie understood the seriousness of what he was asking. "You also need to finish school, whether that's college or a trade, so you can support yourself."

"I'd need to have a job?" Jaimie asked, the excitement in his eyes fading.

"How else do you think you would pay for your condo?"

"Don't elder vampires fund their children?"

"Well, sometimes, for short periods," I said. "I existed with an elder vampire who funded me a few years. However, during the time, I existed as a girl. I had a private tutor. I was expected to do my schoolwork, go through the initiation program to learn to be a modern vampire, keep my room clean, and help his thralls with the dishes and laundry. Then I went to U'dub and worked as a file clerk for a few years before opening my business.

"And of course, there's also the eternity of taxes to think about."

"You have to pay taxes?"

"In this world, nothing is certain, except death and taxes," I said.

"But you didn't die," Jaimie said.

"I died screaming, but then I was Reborn," I said. "As are all vampires."

"Oof," Jaimie said.

"If you do join the initiation program, toss whatever romantic ideas you have about vampirism. Otherwise, your undeath will end quickly."

"You..."

I forced open his mind. This time, I wanted him to feel the tiny footsteps of a million bugs crawling over his brain of a domination spell. "Did you kill Persimmon?"

He twisted his neck around and dragged his nails through his scalp. "Nooo."

"Did Josh?"

"NO. I mean, I don't know."

Now I knew he wasn't the killer, I let Jaimie glimpse the fear I felt due to all the vampires who hated my youth. I showed him the body of a young man who came to the coven and tried to film vampires last summer. His father wanted to change him; he accidentally killed him in a moment of bloodlust. I showed him one of my honored brothers who did not make the transformation rotting from the inside out. I showed him what if felt like being burned alive, aware with one's creator as he burned.

Then I let Jaimie go. With eyes wide with terror and his hair falling into his face, he scrambled out of the office.

Carlos was at the door frowning. He glanced toward Jaimie as he dashed out.

"He wanted to be a vampire. I'm guessing he doesn't now," I said. Looking at the doorway, a spark of inspiration slipped into my brain.

Carlos: Get any sleep?

"No." I glanced around him to make sure no one was in hearing range. Then thought better of it. I texted: **Coming up with a theory.**

I can't believe someone would murder someone over something so small. I just have to prove it. We don't have a murder weapon. Is there any evidence I can use to play them?

Carlos: **Zoe's shoe print matched the person using the back door as the entrance and exit.**

People moved in and out. People went where they were not supposed to go. I realized what was missing. If it wasn't magic had not opened a door, and it wasn't forced, then there had to be a key.

Chapter 16

2:30 PM

"**L**OOK, YOU CAN'T KEEP US HERE," ZOE said. "You are infringing on our rights."

I had to trap the guilty party somehow. Otherwise, they were going to escape all together. It was time to make a play. I didn't know if it would work, hell I never did, but I had to give it a shot.

"I appreciate how much everyone has hung around today... It has come to my attention that there have been several crimes in this store. And it is likely whoever killed Persimmon embezzled..."

I expected some rise in heart rates due to physiological response to the stress of the situation and the caffeine everyone had consumed while I was collecting clues. However, Hannah's pulse skyrocketed.

"Now, the evidence shows Persimmon was possibly impaled on a straw, but if she were impaled on a straw, that means the murderer must have thumbs. The cats are innocent. No one, and I mean no one, Basilla, will harm them. I will destroy something you care about if you do."

"Over a cat?" Craig snapped.

"Over an innocent life," I said.

I went on. "Now if someone could not plug the hole of the straw, the straw would break before it impaled anyone, but this wouldn't." I picked up a barista spoon. "And one's missing."

For a twenty-year-old woman at rest in a chair, Hannah was extremely stressed or about to have a heart attack. She was guilty. Now to prove it.

"We discovered someone has been using the back door as an egress and exit. It's not always locked. And someone's boots that match the impression on the back door, going in and out."

I turned to Zoe.

"I knew you were trying to frame one of us," Zoe said. Her gaze bounced among her friends as if she expected them to support her.

Hannah was suddenly glad Zoe's shoes had gum on them.

"You used the back door?"

"What. No!" Zoe said.

"We have evidence you do," I said with just the hint of a domination spell. "Tell me why. We can work this out together."

"I vape. I swear I only poke my head out the backdoor to get a hit. It's tough to quit."

"I understand. My progenitor and I gave up smoking in the '70s," I said. "But don't worry, I knew you didn't do it. In fact, I have a pretty good idea…"

Suddenly Hannah stood up and held up a crucifix towards me. "Shut your lying mouth, vampire."

"Now isn't that a pretty thing," I said.

"That doesn't hurt you?" Jaimie asked.

"Why would it? I was baptized as a Catholic. So, Hannah, you have something you want to share with the group?"

Jaimie started to talk again, but Zoe silenced him with a "Shut your mouth" look in her eyes.

Every muscle in Hannah's body shivered as I walked towards her. She tried to block her thoughts so I just said what she knew. "Want to share how you stabbed Persimmon to hide your stealing?" I said.

"No, I didn't. I was studying just like I said I was." Hannah cried. "What, I was!"

"I'm sure you were studying, but that's not all you did last night..."

"I'm going to call the cops. I'm going to post this all over social media. How you people are trying to frame me!"

I was so glad I had not wasted any energy trying to read minds. "No, you won't, because pixies, kobolds, and all the other peoples not of typical size will hear about what you did if you post anything."

"You can't prove any of this!" Hannah screamed.

"Of course, I can. Check her keys," I said. "Hannah has a key to the front door."

"That's your proof?" Hannah shouted, but her flesh took on a distinctly undead pallor. Zoe grabbed Hannah's keys and passed them to Josh.

There were four keys on the ring, one was a car key, but the other three were keys to deadbolts.

Josh inserted the first key in the front door. It didn't fit. The second key did. He turned it. The bolt slid back and forth.

In most fictional mysteries, I have read, watched, or listened to, the crowd does not devolve into chaos when the murderer is named, but the murderer, discovering they are caught, confesses. I have found in real life that wasn't the case.

"How did you get that key?" Weyna screamed. "Give it back!"

Josh removed it from the keyring and placed it on the table near Weyna.

Hannah tried to touch Josh's hand. "You have to understand why I did it, don't you, Josh?"

"Don't ever speak to me again," Josh said, ripping their arm away from her hands. "How could you? We trusted you!"

Hannah tried to run for the door.

Airie backed away as Basilla started to buzz

Weyna cradled the stolen key in her arms. "I trusted her. I thought she was a friend to the pixies. How could I hire her? How could I?"

"It'll be okay, Mom," Meadow said. She and Craig went to comfort her.

In the chair beside Josh, Zoe's eyes brimmed with tears. She felt personally betrayed. She looked down at her feet. Furious for trusting Hannah, for liking her. Furious that her footprint broke the case. I understood feeling many ways about someone.

Beside Zoe, Jaimie's mouth hung open in a stunned expression. He didn't move until Zoe cried openly. Jaimie put a hand on her arm. Zoe leaned towards him, he put his arm around her.

Basilla divebombed Hannah. She grabbed a mug off the table and threw it at her. Coffee splattered. The mug smashed in three large pieces on the floor. She was trying to get her away from the door.

Basilla grabbed a sharp piece and held it like a weapon.

"Stop!" I shouted. My direction was unheeded. "Basilla, stop."

"It was an accident," Hannah screamed.

Carlos roared. His direction was heeded. Everyone stopped moving. The college students went one way; the pixies flew the other.

"Now, please, everyone calm down," I said.

"What are you going to do with her?" Weyna shouted.

"I just solve the crimes. I have no jurisdiction over the pixies, humans or witches," I said. "The humans can call their police for you, I guess. She stole from the store. Josh can file charges on your behalf."

Basilla threw another coffee mug across the room. It shattered against the wall. "Do something!"

"What do you want me to do?"

"You could eat her. Eat her to shut her two-faced lying mouth," Basilla screamed.

I thought, *lying mouth?* So Basilla knows something. Or suspects Persimmon wasn't an innocent. *This wasn't random.*

Basilla kept shouting: "You and Carlos, that's what you do."

I enjoyed the feeling of the frightened, angry emotions and heartbeats falling against my. It piqued my bloodlust. Even still, I wasn't stupid enough to kill Hannah in front of the others. Jaimie might be interested to see blood fall, but most people of all types were squeamish. "That is not what we do."

"We can't have our vengeance against a human. Our laws against capital punishment bind us. Why won't you help us?" Weyna asked.

"Look, you claimed that you are understaffed," I said.

"But we can't have a pixie killer working for us either. And she stole from us," Meadow cried.

"Then fire her."

Hannah grabbed her keys from the table and ran out.

"So, now what?" Meadow asked.

Carlos waved goodbye.

"I was asked to solve the crime. I have," I said. "Hannah was stealing from the company, mostly little things and small amounts of money. And as she said, she got frightened and killed Persimmon. Good day. I will see you tonight for our free coffee."

Chapter 17

3:00 PM

T HE SKY HAD OPENED UP WHEN WE HAD been in the cat café. Icy raindrops fell from the gray sky, and rivulets of water ran towards downtown. Silly locals we were, we never carried an umbrella, at least, not for the rain.

"Want me to walk you to your car?" I asked.

Carlos nodded.

The damp sunk into my sneakers, and my feet grew chilly. Tucking my hoodie around me, I fought the urge to run. Only a few humans were on the street; I could not pinpoint why I felt threatened, yet I felt as if I was putting myself in some ancient, nameless peril, and Carlos was in danger due to my presence.

Washington was an at-will employment state, and he'd write he is a grown-ass man and makes his own decisions. Still, I got him in this business and felt responsible for him. Maybe it was a universal thing to feel responsible for someone that you found undead and comatose under a pool table. "Something in the air feels wrong," I said.

He scribbled on his pad. You still think the cats are safe.

"Yes. I meant I'm sensing Bill again."

Carlos: Think he's here?

I opened my mind to my creator. He was nearby, but not hiding under the next tree or my apartment. I shook my head. I wished I could ask Carlos to stay the day with me.

Carlos: You've been up all day. You're exhausted.

Forcing my eyes not to blink, I asked, "Want to skip work tonight? I might just go to Derrik's early."

Carlos nodded. He closed his eyes, tilted his head, and mimicked snoring. Then he pointed at me, bared his teeth, and mimicked biting.

I laughed. "Yeah, I'm going to take care of that problem as soon as I can."

Carlos: Be safe and take care. See you Tuesday night.

"You too. See you."

With a wave, he climbed into his car and pulled out of the parking lot.

I still had to do something about Hannah, but first, I must resist the temptation of a cozy bed. I would clean my bathroom, do the laundry, and prepare my home for Derrik's visit. Once finished, I would dressed in layers of warm black clothing. I did not know how long this hunt would take, but it would take patience.

Chapter 18

6:00 PM

WEARING A BLACK GORE-TEX JACKET and letting my jeans grow damp from the rain, I stood in the darkness and enjoyed looking at the Christmas lights from windows created rainbow patterns on the wet pavement. Together the pattern mimicked a Christmas tree. Downtown, the street trees were decorated with white lights and bows. Queen Anne sparkled. I could see each of the twelve hundred lights twinkling in rows on top of the Space Needle. I loved Seattle during the holidays.

Finally, Hannah left her apartment and walked toward Broadway. I followed.

The young woman glanced back over her shoulder. Her breathing accelerated as did her heartbeat. Sweat dewed her soft complexion. She jammed her hand into her jacket pockets, searching for a weapon. Hannah found her keys and pressed them between her fingers. The woman's anxiety shifted to terror. Her heart battered against her ribs, exciting my bloodlust.

I never killed a pixie killer, but I had put down other fiends. I could make a person with enemies disappear, but that wouldn't do for a well-liked college student in this day and age. She was probably on Instagram, Snapchat, and Twitter plus Tinder or whatever dating app she used. Too many people would notice she was gone. Too many people would look, and it might come back on Weyna and her family.

I pulled Hannah into an alley, which smelled of fetid, rotting garbage, and urine.

Good. That would add to Hannah's fear. No one wanted to die around garbage. Even if Hannah couldn't see them, she would know that there were rats, insects, and spiders, and other things she could not see.

The young woman's blonde ponytail whipped through the air as she attempted to punch me with her makeshift weapon. I easily dodged. With my vampire strength, I overpowered the other woman and pushed her against the brick wall. I knocked her hand to make her drop her keys and bit deep into her neck. I tasted the sheen of sweat on her flesh, but I felt no guilt for the woman's fear.

Hannah's iron-rich blood was like many young people's salty and opulent on the tongue. I wanted it all, but I held back.

I pressed my free hand against the rough, pitted, hundred-year-old brick. I detected it came from the Cougar Mountain factory. With the blood in my mouth and a hand on ancient earth, I saw through Hannah's life. She had a mother and father who loved her, who wanted her to succeed. And I was right about the social media presence.

Hannah screamed, then whimpered as she weakened. "Persimmon was just a pixie."

"I wouldn't talk like that. I'm just a vampire," I said.

"But she wasn't what they all thought. It was a lie. She

wasn't any better than me. She was taking half," Hannah cried.

I drew my head back and met the woman's eyes. "I know. I'm a mind reader, remember? Also, I saw how Basilla was trying to shut you up."

I took another sip, growing stronger with the ingested blood. I forced a mental connection. It was easy using Hannah's mortal fear.

"You murdered to hide your petty crime, so you've until the end of the semester to get out of Seattle," I said.

"But my scholarship..." Hannah gasped. "And my lease isn't up until June."

"You have lost any right to live in my city."

"It's not your city."

I knocked her into the brick wall and hissed, "Say that again. It is mine. I claimed it long ago. The ancient vampires don't care, and no lesser vampire can stand against me."

I slapped my hand over the young woman's mouth and bit down again. When Hannah weakened, I dominated her mind. Fearing I would exsanguinate her, she didn't fight.

"Where do your parents live?" I asked, carefully establishing her influence.

"Wenatchee."

"You will go back to Wenatchee."

"My scholarship! Do you know how hard I worked to get where I am?" Tears sprang to Hannah's eyes.

"Hard enough to murder someone." I lowered my voice.

Hannah's head flinched back as I blew my cold breath on the open wound, reinforcing the mental connection. "But you will return to Wenatchee. You will find a job and live there contentedly."

Hannah's mind still fought against me. I sensed Bill and the ancient vampire getting closer. "My parents won't understand."

"You miss your family. You miss the small town you grew up in. Now when is your last class?" I asked,

"December 12th," Hannah said, the light in her eyes growing dim.

"You will leave Seattle after your last class. You will have until December 15th, and then I will check on you. You don't want me to find you in Seattle."

"I will leave Seattle," she said, domination complete.

"Tell your roommate tonight," I said.

"Tell my roommate tonight," Hannah repeated.

"Call your mother tonight. Tell her you are coming home forever."

"I will call my mother tonight and tell her I am coming home forever," Hannah echoed.

"When I seek you out, if you are still in Seattle, you will die. You must leave Seattle."

Hannah nodded. "I understand."

"You will remember your task and the fear of death, but you will not remember me."

I forced a picture of Hannah lying with her throat torn open in an abandoned alley. She would die unable to breathe, unable to cry for help.

"Now go."

Hannah dashed away. She did not look back.

I walked back to the street. I didn't want to meet Bill

in a urine-filled alley. A wave of grief and fear splashed over my heart, but I turned east and waved at two figures walking toward me.

"Hello, Bill, Gaius."

Chapter 19

7:25 PM

"**A**M I NO LONGER DAD?" BILL STRODE towards me with a slight frown on his face.

My stomach hardened as the old feelings came flooding back. I had loved, hated, and feared him in equal measure. Until the other vampires found me, I called him Dad or Daddy and did my best to placate his anger by mimicking scenes from movies since I did not remember my human father.

"It's been a long time."

That response felt safest. Hannah's delicious blood rose in the back of my throat, I wanted to vomit. I pushed it down. I would face my father and ancient ancestor on my feet and without retching.

William Caruso, aka Bill, had only existed as a vampire for fourteen years longer than me. He was physically stronger than I due to the fact he started his undead existence as a full-grown man, and I was a girl, but in vampire prowess we were probably close to the same. He had passed down Derrik's mind-reading abilities to me. He would sense my emotions. I wasn't sure how ancient Gaius was or all his powers, but centuries ago, he told Agata he was already a vampire when the Prophet of Judah walked the earth. And he was a documented clairvoyant.

"Why did you let that girl live?" Gaius asked.

"Because I am not an idiot," I said. "Young popular college student will be looked for. When I choose to kill her, I will do it when it won't come back to my door."

I did not see a waiting car, but they obviously came from somewhere. They both wore jeans and sportscoats, slightly too nice for the Fleece and Gore-tex-wearing casualness of Seattle. Their dark curly hair ruffed in the wet winter air. It was strange how much the two vampires resembled each other, which meant they also resembled me. My Italian descended looks were one of the reasons I was chosen to be Bill's daughter.

However, Bill was almost a foot taller than me and built like a brick house. Gaius was not tall for a man, especially compared to the men of the twenty-first century, but his broad shoulders and muscular arms made him seem larger. Gaius's hazel eyes were closer to green, where Bill's were closer to brown, but otherwise, they looked like they might be brothers. Though they both wore the same uncanny smiles, their expressions were not friendly. I admit I wondered if my existence would end.

"How long will you wait?" Gaius asked.

"Until I feel it is safe for me and the coven," I said.

Gaius laughed, but the sound was one of mocking rather than joy. "An arbitrary measurement."

"When I stole you from your mother, you weren't looked for," Bill said.

"I was, but my mom didn't have today's resources

or social media. If you expect to live in the Paper Flower Consortium's city, you better be smart, my honored creator and ancestor. It's a new world." Fearing that might sound like a challenge, I changed the subject. "You are both looking well."

"As are you, though you should have died decades ago," Gaius said.

"Some could say the same about you. Yet, here we are."

"I heard you were running with a zombie," Bill said. "And we saw the man today, correct?"

"Yes."

I both wished Carlos was there at that moment and glad he wasn't. I wasn't sure what he might do, but I couldn't risk this reunion getting physical. There was nothing I could really do if an ancient vampire wanted to rumble. *If I meet my final death tonight, I'll die fighting.*

"Is he your lover?"

"Just a friend. This form doesn't allow for long romantic relationships." I crossed my arms. I wanted to ask, "What are you doing here?" Instead, my voice warbled as the real question rose to my lips, "How did you escape?"

"Vampires are notoriously hard to kill."

"But they dismembered you. I felt it. And I felt you burning," I said. A single tear fell then. I brushed it away. *Why do I have to start crying?*

"You did feel me dismembered and burnt by the rising sun, but you never felt me meet my final death, Daughter. I had a trusted thrall to move me after the vampires finished their work. I was quite indisposed for decades."

"But Aldo thought you were dead. He hated me most

of the time because you met your final death," I said.

"He gave you his blood without quarrel?"

"Yes."

"Then, he served his purpose."

I refused to shiver from those frosty words. Aldo had loved Bill as his vampire master; Bill never loved anyone. *Not me, not Derrik, not Laurence, not the coven.*

"I removed Aldo's memory of the events. Otherwise, you would have known Bill wasn't dead," Gaius said. "He didn't fight it. He wanted to save Bill no matter what the cost to himself."

Bill reached for my shoulder, but I stepped back from him. He frowned. "You still don't love me?"

"You made me a vampire. I love you and grieved for you, but I still haven't forgotten how things were between us."

"To my shame, but Derrik was obviously a good father."

I sniffed. "He was good to me, but he always said he was my mentor and is my honored brother."

"He would." Gaius rolled his eyes. "*Mortacci tua!*" (Your dead ancestors!)

Since Derrik created Bill, I wondered if Bill would say anything about the slur against our shared ancestor, but instead, Bill's brow was furrowed and his jaw clenched. A bolt of fear raced into my chest. I automatically dropped my eyes to his fist to see if it would fly. It didn't.

"Derrik is your descendant," I said.

"Not by choice," Gaius said. "Of all the vampires from this insufferable bloodline, only Bill is worthy to walk beside me. You might be."

"I spent the past seventy-years exploring our gifts," Bill said. "I learned many things. I know darkness. I could show you."

I could not deny the temptation. "Can you turn into a bat?"

"No."

"Mist?"

"No one knows such things."

"Can you fly?"

"And so could you if you harnessed the power of darkness," Bill said.

"Does this darkness make you content?" I asked.

"No, nothing can make me content, but I exist outside the coven rules, which helps."

"It's why I live outside the coven, but I am a member. Why did you seek me out?"

"I missed my daughter. It's Christmas time." Bill said. That was partially why he was there, but not any part of why Gaius was there.

"And you were watching me today?"

"Indeed, we are staying downtown and felt you rise. We wanted to see you at work before I wasted any time looking into your services. Now tell us, why did you help the pixies?" Gaius asked.

I ignored the bugs which were crawling through her mind. "Free coffee for a year. There is no need to dominate me. We are having a civilized conversation."

Gaius did not break the domination spell.

"I could kill the pixies," Bill said.

I pulled a card out of my back pocket and banished the

bugs from my mind with the movement. "And I would clean up the mess.

"It will be a seven-thousand-dollar job, at least. I accept cash, debit, and credit cards. Personal cheques if drafted from an established vampire bank."

"To pick up bodies no bigger than a hand?" Gaius asked.

"And close down the business, fix anything that needs fixing and pay off or dominate anyone, you ancient idiots, show yourselves too," I said.

"You used to have more respect for your elders," Bill said.

"I have plenty of respect for elders worthy of respect. Ancient vampires are often too sure of themselves. They take risks," I said. "As do the vampires who walk beside them, *Dad.*"

"So you do care?" Bill asked, with a hint of a smile widening his lips.

"My feelings are my own...

I found myself rambling due to the domination on my mind. "You survived, but not even a phone call. You knew I was with Derrik. Why didn't you call us?"

"I couldn't call. I was in literal pieces. It took many years for my body to heal from dismemberment. I did check on you from time to time. Every year, I found you were more worthy to walk beside us."

"Well, I have plans with Derrik this weekend!" My words sound more petulant, even to my own ears. *Why do I have to feel this?*

"What plans?" Bill asked.

Gaius narrowed his eyes and interrupted before I could answer. "I tire of this reunion. I have a job for you after the new New year, but before the old New Year."

I turned to him. Of course, Gaius still remembers the old New Year. He lived with the old calendar longer. "I know. You want me to read someone's mind?"

"Yes."

"Someone powerful. You don't want to chance Bill's existence, but I am expendable. Plus if he reads me, you can ensure that I am being truthful to you. Is this job local?"

"No, but your travel will be arranged to your satisfaction."

"And payment?"

"Money and the gift of flight. You see, ancient vampires pay much better than pixies."

Flight. My heart beat quickly. I was showing my hand. "I..." I needed to stop my eagerness. "I need to speak to my attorney."

Bill took a step back. He crossed his arms, but I saw how his hand squeezed his arm.

Gaius laughed. "And you will seek Agata's advice no doubt."

"Yes," I didn't see any point to lie.

He flashed a cold smile. "Don't take too long. What's Derrik's Secondborn's name?" He snapped his fingers and looked to the sky for a moment. "Ryan Jones. He also can read minds or so I'm told."

"Is your mark merfolk or sea serpent?"

"No, another vampire," Gaius said.

"Then Ryan isn't the one you want. He'll give away

your game. He's a qualified marine biologist, but nothing more."

Gaius's mocking laugh was back. "The sad thing is while I know you are protecting your honored brother; you are also telling the truth. Your bloodline progenitor would also give up the game as you say."

"As I said, I have plans this weekend, but please write up the details of your proposal and email, fax, or mail it to my office at the Paper Flower Consortium. The address is on the card. I will have Derrik and Jakub look over it on Monday. I suspect unless your offer is generous, they will suggest a counter-offer." I handed Gaius my card.

"Do you always follow your elders' advice?"

"Legal and financial advice are benefits of coven membership. I pay my dues, I ought to use my allotted benefits."

Gaius laughed again. "Bill was right about you. You don't disappoint. Go in peace."

"Norma," Bill said softly. "Is Ryan...? He and Derrik seem much alike in personality. Or, at least, they do in your head."

"Ryan and Derrik are and have always been simply friends. Derrik couldn't bear having another offspring who broke his heart."

"I wasn't good for him any more than I was a good father to you. Will you tell him I exist?"

Bill might not have loved Derrik in the way Derrik needed, but he had loved him in his way. Indeed, Bill always considered Derrik to be an angel of sorts. Beautiful, ethereal, but no fun to exist with as a partner.

Gaius, no doubt, was better suited to Bill.

"I will," I said.

"Before the rest of the coven?"

"I always planned to speak to Derrik first. He deserves to know and weep in privacy."

"Thank you," Bill said.

"Will you do something for me in good faith to our future possible business arrangement?" I asked.

"What's that?"

"Leave Laurence Roch be."

"What do you know of Larry? Has he finally joined the coven?" Bill asked.

"No, he was my tutor when I was a girl..."

"So it was he who taught you to hunt?"

I laughed. "No, he taught me geometry and grammar. And he is under my protection as my honored brother. He mourned you deeply."

Gaius snapped, "A thousand Gods, are there any vampires in Seattle not under your protection?"

"You," I said.

Gaius laughed.

Bill handed me a black card made of thick paper. "I am glad to see you still care about people that no one else does. You're the one good thing I created."

I watched as Bill and Gaius rose in the air and disappeared into the darkness. I looked down at the card and read the gold embossed lettering.

William Thomas Caruso
Vampire

Followed by a phone number and a hotel room at the Four Seasons. Gaius and Bill really did travel first class.

December 6, 2019

FRIDAY

Chapter 20

Midnight

SITTING IN MY VAN, I WATCHED THE WAVES break against the rocky shoreline of Alki. I had driven to West Seattle to relax in the late night quiet, but the drive had not brought me tranquility. All the caffeine and Hannah's blood had given me too much energy. Knowing Bill was undead and in Seattle made my mind spiral. I felt as if something had been stolen. Maybe, my confidence. Maybe, my knowledge of my place in vampire society. My home in Seattle.

I loved the city. The reflection of skyscrapers adorned with Christmas lights danced in the water. Columbia Tower's LED trim was red and green. The Smith Tower's orb was green. Tiny raindrops fell on the windshield, obscuring her view. Another caused the first to cascade.

Bats occasionally flew over me. I would like to fly away right now. *With flight,* I thought. *I might really be a superhero.*

I still hadn't slept. Maybe I should sleep before making any decisions, but I didn't feel like going back to my condo. I never really believed the Paper Flower Consortium had successfully executed Bill. I had been right. What would the rest of the coven say? Would they be surprised? Which vampires in Seattle he knew were undead. *Jakub? Maybe. Derrik? No.*

"I shouldn't feel like this! He took away my humanity." I found I did not care about that. I had been a vampire too long.

"We spent only months together, and he beat me several times," I shouted toward the water, knowing no one could hear my rage. "He broke my ribs. He left bruises."

Bloody tears filled my eyes and turned my vision red, masking my view further. "He took me away from my mother." I still did miss my mom.

I clicked on the phone-icon on my dash. "Call Derrik" and before the voice could confirm the request. I quickly said, "Cancel."

I pinched my eyes shut. *I have to tell him in person... and this can't wait.* I wasn't dressed like a vampire, but I stored my vintage dresses in the office.

Glancing in the rearview mirror, I half-expected to see Bill and Gaius rise from the waves. I put my van in reverse and backed out of the parking spot.

I drove to the Paper Flower Consortium. I changed out of my dirty clothes, showered, and dressed mostly like a vampire ought. This time, my vampire costume was a gray and black plaid dress with a matching gray sweater. To modernize the outfit and make it Christmas-y, I slipped on black leggings with a pattern of tiny gray reindeer.

Though I might go through the private interiors and peek through the glazing in the window to see if he was alone, I went through the public side. I said hello to Derrik's executive assistant, a human woman named Suzan. I made it a policy to be polite and respectful to all of Derrik's assistants.

Suzan told me that Derrik was in and rang into his office.

Derrik took one look at me. "You have some bad news."

For a moment, I did not know what to say. I could not organize my thoughts. Obviously, he knew something was up. Or I wouldn't be standing there in one of my old dresses.

I blurted out: "I don't know how to tell you this, or even if I should tell you this, but Bill survived."

"Norma..."

I pulled the card out and tried to hand it to him.

"I saw him tonight with Gaius. Look in my mind if you don't believe me."

Derrik eyes didn't leave my face. He didn't bother to read my mind or take the card. He gasped and made a choking sound. Then silence. He loosened his tie and took off his jacket. If he weren't a vampire, I would have thought Derrik was hyperventilating. I guided him to the overstuffed leather couch in front of a bookcase packed with massive tomes.

"Are you all right?" I asked. "I didn't mean to hurt you."

Derrik did not answer as he sagged into the couch.

In this moment of silence, the room spun.

I had been in Derrik's office a thousand times, but now it seemed like a stranger's room. The man who raised me seemed like a stranger too. I hoped Derrik would want to remain my family. He choose me once, but I was not sure he would choose me now I didn't need him anymore. Bill had been a different man to Derrik than he had been to me. Derrik had loved him. They had been lovers. *Derrik will want to see him. Maybe I shouldn't have told him…*

"Bill couldn't have survived," Derrik whispered.

Even though his voice was low, his old Victorian Cockney accent, which he hated and had worked hard to disguise, changed his diction. It often did when he was upset. "He was dismembered and tied…."

I tucked my knees underneath me as I sat down beside him. "He endured the torture. He exists as you and I do. Gaius saved him."

"Are you all right?" His a's became long and shrill to my American ears. His skin wrinkled around his eyes as he searched my face.

"Yes."

He gripped my hands a little too tightly. "He didn't injure you?"

"No. He and Gaius have a job and offered to teach me to fly in payment."

Derrik's hands dropped to his lap. "To fly?" He slouched. "I should've known he would have had some plan. I don't know how to feel…how did he look?"

"Sort of the same. He was wearing a nice sportscoat and jeans, leather shoes, leather gloves, and a fedora. I'm sure he has money — or is existing on Gaius's money. Maybe he's working for him, or possibly they are lovers. I was too emotional to ask intelligent questions."

I went over the entire conversation with Derrik, trying hard not to leave anything out—even the minor threat towards Ryan.

"You are tempted." He tried to loosen his tie. Finding it loose, he twisted his wedding ring.

"Aren't you?"

"No. This is my existence, and I am happy with it," Derrik said. I heard the slight rebuke in his tone.

"Are you worried about Ryan and Fern freaking out?" I asked.

"Well, they will need to know about this as it may have to do with Fern's future bloodline decision, but until you mentioned it, I didn't think of them at all. I was distraught Bill took some vengeance on you."

"He didn't touch me."

Derrik buried his face in his hands. "Norma's Cleaning Service didn't become the most profitable subdivision by rejecting clients. But you won't trust him?" He paused before he added his habitual, "my lamb." It was hard to understand with the accent, but the way he said those two words sounded like a strangled question.

"Neither of them," I said.

"Good." He took a shaky breath. "Are you about to tell me you rather spend your holidays with your father?"

"No." I quickly hugged him about the neck. When I released him, I retrieved a handkerchief from the little box on his end table. "I want to spend the holidays with you."

"He loves you. You know he does. He fought for your existence…"

I handed him the handkerchief.

Choosing my words carefully, I said, "I still feel all those things I felt before for him. But he's not my dad. I know you won't like to hear these words, but if I had a dad that was you, not him."

Derrik gave me a sad smile and wiped his eyes. "You aren't angry for all the times you told me you sensed Bill and I told you he had met his final death? Because you were right."

"I'm embarrassed to say so, but I was mostly worried you'd go out into the darkness to find Bill. Or worse."

"Why would you think that?"

"Bill is your Firstborn. You've often told me a vampire couldn't help but love their creations. And your heart longs to see him again. "

"I am ecstatic he is undead. I still love my Firstborn, but I don't know if I can ever forgive him." He rubbed his forehead as he closed his eyes. He didn't want to relive the brutal memories any more than I did. "He adored you, yet refused to unlearn his human sins."

"I'm not a little girl anymore. He doesn't hit people he considers equal."

Derrik hesitantly took my hand. I felt him relax as I leaned into his shoulder.

"What do you think the others will say?"

"I don't know. Ryan and most of Loretta and Charles's descendants never knew Bill. It's possible they won't understand the elders' concern."

"Is it possible they will want to prune Bill's branch of the bloodline from the coven? Finally, get rid of the Shame?"

"Doubtful. Too many would protect you. Loretta's bloodline remembers the services you provided to Xiao as of late. Anyone who decides not to remember wouldn't want to lose the money Norma's Cleaning Service brings into the coven."

Hoping to cheer him, I asked, "Did you still want to go Christmas shopping and decorate the tree and all the other things we had planned for the weekend?"

A tentative smile grew on his face. "If you do."

"Yes, I do. I washed the quilt you like and put it into your coffin, went to the market, so I'm ready for you to stay the day. May I assume you still have no idea what to get Pascaline for Christmas?"

He chuckled. His voice returned to normal. "No clue. However, now the gift should be even more special. She will not take this news well."

"Want me to go read her mind for clues?"

"If you would, my lamb. She's in the library with Loretta, I think."

"Don't worry, I'm on the case.

"If I have to, I'll peek into her closet and see what's getting worn down. Or speak to her new thrall—what's her name again?"

"Madison."

I slipped my arms around his shoulders and gave him a quick hug then jumped off the couch.

Death, dismemberment, and Bill's continued survival didn't change how Derrik felt about me. Dead pixies, guilty humans, witches, werewolves, merfolk, sea serpents, and everybody else I faced on a nightly basis didn't either. Nothing that happened tonight changed us.

Or the fact, we had much to do before Christmas.

The End

Pecan Tarts

This is a recipe my family enjoys around Christmas. I hope you enjoy eating them and don't just push straws through them as an experiment.

Crust
2 1/2 cups all-purpose flour, plus extra for rolling
2 sticks (8 oz unsalted butter) very-cold, cut into 1/2 inch cubes
1 teaspoon salt
1 teaspoon sugar
6 to 8 tablespoons cold water
Filling
1 cup Karo Dark Corn Syrup
3 eggs
1 cup sugar
2 tablespoons butter, melted
1 teaspoon pure vanilla extract
8 ounces pecans

Crust: Put flour, sugar, and salt into the bowl of a food processor and pulse a couple times to mix. Add butter slowly, pulsing several times after each addition until the largest pieces of butter are about the size of large peas. Slowly add water, a tablespoon at a time, pulsing once or twice after each addition until the dough just barely begins to hold together. Carefully empty the crumbly dough mixture from the food processor on to a clean, dry, flat surface. Gather the mixture in a large mounds. Divide the dough mixture into two even-sized mounds. Use your hands and knead each mound just enough to form each one into a disk. Do not over-knead! You should just knead enough so that the dough holds together without cracks. Sprinkle each disk with a little flour, wrap each one in plastic wrap, and refrigerate for one hour or up to 2 days. Remove dough from refrigerator. Let sit at room temperature for 5-10 minutes in order to soften just enough to make rolling out a bit easier. Roll out dough until 1/8 inch thick. Cut in circles. Lightly spray a standard-size 12-cup muffin tin with vegetable oil Carefully place crust onto a greased muffin tin and press down so that it lines the bottom and sides. Trim the dough if necessary and flute with fork or fingers if you like. Preheat Oven to 350 F.
Filling: Mix corn syrup, eggs, sugar, butter and vanilla using a spoon. Pour filling into pie crusts. Top with pecans
Bake on center rack of oven for 25 - 30 minutes.
Remove from oven. Let sit in pan for 15 minutes to firm up and then remove and cool on wire rack.

RECIPE TIPS:
Baked tarts freeze well and also hold for three days in the fridge, wrapped in waxed paper and then foil. To refresh, bake the tart at 325°F until warm, 5 min. if refrigerated; 10-12 min. if frozen.

Prologue

DEAR DIARY,

HI. MY NAME IS NORMA MAE Rollins, and I don't want to die again. It hurt so much the first time.

I found you in my new desk in my new home. Vampires love to document everything. Their library holds many diaries. I'm pretty sure they will keep you if I fill you out. If they destroy me, I won't be forgotten.

I was born at home on February 8, 1938.

I am fourteen, the only child of Margret Anne Rollins, née Rici, and her deceased husband, Robert Michael Joseph Rollins. I don't remember my real dad, but I loved my mom.

My vampire dad, Bill, plucked me from my life when he stole me from my friends.

The Paper Flower Consortium in Seattle took me from Bill. I wish Bill told me more about the coven vampires. Before he faced execution, he had said, I needed to be strong, and no matter what, I must stay with Derrik, his progenitor.

For now, the coven agrees. I don't have a choice. The coven doesn't trust me. They think I'll break a pipe or something.

Wait. Maybe I shouldn't write it's my home.

It's Derrik's home.

He might not like if I claim it. I have to be careful until I figure what sets him off. I keep scrolling through films with vampires or rich, fancy people. None of it fits.

I don't know who I'm supposed to be here.

I admit Derrik's been pretty nice since we met tonight, but his bloody tears are chilling. His sorrow washes over me and I want to weep too. He loved Bill. Now he's stuck with me. I wish I could go home to my mom.

I guess I ought to start with the night I became a vampire.

Chapter 1

DEAR DIARY,
THE LAST NIGHT OF MY LIFE, I felt more alive than I ever had in my fourteen years. The stars twinkled above the grassy field outside Issaquah. The air was perfumed with summer grasses, pine, and fruit trees.

Careful I didn't interrupt Janice and Perry or Betty and Matt, I slowed my pace to let Teddy catch me. Every inch of skin felt alive as he squeezed my wrist. He playfully pulled me close. His lips tasted of beer and Wrigley's Doublemint gum as they brushed against mine. I wanted to kiss Teddy forever.

Still, our lips parted.

I giggled and darted away like the other girls did. The girls ran. The boys gave chase. I did the same. After all, one had to be careful not to ruin one's reputation.

Icy fingers, too big to be Teddy's, gripped my arms.

The Fuzz, I thought.

The sheriff would call Mom. I'd had a few sips of beer and smoked, but I wasn't blitzed. At worse, Mom would be "very disappointed" and give me extra chores.

My feet lifted from the ground. Wind bit the bare flesh of my arms, legs, and face. Branches whipped past me in frenzied movement. Nothing made logical sense. I seemed to fly underneath the dark shape which held me.

I was dropped onto the concrete floor of somewhere cold that smelled of rotting meat and filth. A vampire's fangs loomed in front of me.

Vampires aren't supposed to be real!

I screamed and struck my assailant with my flashlight. His pale lip split open and quickly stitched back together. He yanked the flashlight from my hand. I protected my throat with my arms, because in the movies, vampires always bite people in the throat.

He punched me.

Dazed, I fell backward into a metal table. He lifted me onto it and rolled me over. I spotted the pit half-filled with rotting bodies sprinkled with lime. Their mottled flesh twisted in bizarre angles. Cloudy eyes stared at the ceiling.

Wild with terror, I kicked out. I felt air. I connected once. He grunted and leaned one hand on my back, pressing me into the metal. With his other hand, he ripped off my shoe and bobby-sock. His fangs pierced my heel. When he reopened his mouth, he whispered something about Achilles.

I tried to lift myself off the metal slab, but the vampire had me pinned. Cold leeched through my summer blouse. My muscles spasmed.

The barn spun. Darkness.

No! Mom'll wake up ... I won't be home ... I'll be a rotting body covered in lye.

He loosened his grip to check his stopwatch. I twisted. With my free leg, I kicked the vampire as hard as I could.

Freed but light-headed, I sat and elbowed him in the chest. Agonizing pain radiated into my arm. Ignoring the throbbing, I punched him in his mouth, maybe his nose.

Blood sprayed onto my face. My eyes teared, burning

with his fiery blood. My lips tasted like copper.

The vampire grabbed me.

With one final burst of strength, I lunged and clamped my teeth onto his hand. Salty, syrupy blood coated my mouth....

Want to read more?
Accident Among Vampires
(OR WHAT WOULD DRACULA DO?)
is available in Paperback and Ebook
and illustrated Hardback!

ABOUT THE AUTHOR

MUCH TO HER CHAGRIN, ELIZABETH Guizzetti discovered she was not a cyborg and growing up to be an otter would be impractical, so began writing stories at age twelve. Three decades later, Guizzetti is an illustrator and author best known for her demon-poodle based comedy, *Out for Souls & Cookies*. She is also the creator of *For the Love of Pancakes, Faminelands* and *Lure* and collaborated with authors on several projects including *A is for Apex* and *The Prince of Artemis V*.

To explore a different aspect of her creativity, she writes science fiction and fantasy. Her debut novel, *Other Systems*, was a 2015 Finalist for the Canopus Award for excellence in Interstellar Fiction. Her short work has appeared in anthologies such as *Wee Folk and The Wise, 99 Tiny Terrors,* and *Cthulhu FhCon*. She has always loved fantasy and horror books: especially vampires. A common theme in much of her work is questionable morality, the meaning of family, and people just trying to get through life no matter what their species. This is why after writing *Immortal House*, Guizzetti went on a writing-spree of vampire books set in the Paper Flower Universe. She set the contemporary books in the series in Seattle because she resides there with her husband and her dog.

To follow her work, check out:
Twitter: @E_Guizzetti
Instagram: Elizabeth_Guizzetti
Facebook Fan Page: Elizabeth.Guizzetti.Author
Webpage: http://elizabethguizzetti.com

Paper Flower Consortium Books:

NORMA'S CLEANING SERVICES MYSTERIES
Death Pulls a Stake Out, 2018
Death Hears a Siren, 2019
Death Sticks a Pixie, 2019

ELDERS OF THE PAPER FLOWER CONSORTIUM
Honor Among Vampires, 2019 (Agata's Story)
Chivalry Among Vampires, 2020 (Jakub's Story)
Accident Among Vampires Or What Would Dracula Do?, 2021 (Norma's Childhood Story)
Immortal House, 2018 (Laurence's Story)
Vampires of the Paper Flower Consortium (Anthology) 2022
Vampires of the Paper Flower Consortium Podcast

COMICS
Faminelands, 2008-2012
Out For Souls & Cookies! 2009 - 2016
Lure, 2011

Legend of Walnut Razorfang

Novels and Novellas
Other Systems
The Light Side of the Moon
The Grove

Illustration Projects
A is for Apex written by Jennifer Brozek
The Prince of Artemis V written by Jennifer Brozek